EDUTAINMENT
Education plus Entertainment

Since the main Character in the play is a Lecturer who is also an ESL Teacher, retired from being a Public Secondary School English Teacher, for stage productions, during the public auditioning period, the Characters that have an education can be opened to those in the same professional occupation.   That is, a real English Teacher can perform the main role of The Professor, especially if they do public lectures and school lectures. It would give the necessary credentials and credibility to the role and to Edutainment for stage theater.

This poetic play is open to collaborative editing to whoever performs the role of The Professor, meaning his lecture notes can be added to the explanations interspersed between the entire play, especially for any lines pertaining to The Professor. Each Production would need to submit any inclusions or changes required along with licensing for performance request forms.

Issues for Discussion

Diversity
Sexuality
Morality
Identity
Intelligence
Creativity
Information
Human Nature
Laws and Rules
Metaphysical

In a collaboration between Education and Entertainment based groups the issues above have to be effectively presented for analysis and discussion. The targeted locations and markets are the schools and the studios, auditoriums and theater stages for public presentations.

For the occupational roles, preference would be given to those already practising in those professions because in reality, art reflects life, life reflects art. It gives more credibility to the performances for those who like reality. They are internally matching their external mental and emotional map, and not merely pretending to be someone. But it takes years to become a Character and perform a Role in life, years of education and practise to be a Teacher or Lawyer. So, if an Actor without that background attempts to play such a role, it may not be believable to an audience.

The poetry provides the fiction, the wording in sonnets, and from the imagined fictional dialogues and monologues of Characters. This is only an attempt to bridge Education with Entertainment, reality with imagination.

Schools are institutions with formal rules restricting human behaviour, sometimes contradicting human nature, especially the primitive instincts, for the purpose of civilizing individuals to suit a Moral Society. Unfortunately, art and entertainment can release repressed desires, contradicting the goals of education. Thus the challenge of creating edutainment balances natural instincts encouraged by arts with civilized expectations of repressing them in schools.

The names and cultural backgrounds of each Character can be changed depending on each Production. Since diversity often relates to race, culture, background, physique and this play would like to include instead of exclude various Performers, depending on the country it is performed in, it can be changed and adapted by prior application for licensing for performance.

The English language is considered an international language spoken in the Commonwealth nations and entire North America where most immigration is directed. Canada and USA are full of diversity and would be the prime market for viewing considering Government policies encourage it, especially in schools.

Diversity changes people. Consider that immigrants from Asia, Europe, Africa and South America entering North America will change, immersed in diversity of various languages, cultures, races. This play reflects this acculturation learning process.

TABLE OF CONTENTS

CHARACTERS

The Professor Lecturer   Helmut Wroth
The Storyteller
The Tourist
The Broadcaster and Technicians
The Trader and Co-Workers
The Teachers
The Lovers
The Leaders   The Queen and The General
The Lawyer
The ESL Students   Mario Lanzones
                      Lei and Chiara

The Administration Staff
The Hecklers
The Guests

Two Stage Versions
In the Full XXX Rated Version Include:
The Prostitute / The Maid
The Gossip
The Chairman   William Von Max
The Assistant

In the Censored Version:
The Poetess

SONNETS USED IN THE POETIC PLAY

[The Professor]
Part 1 The Language Lessons

Part 2 The Characters Lessons

Part 3 Conclusion

CENSORED VERSION ONLY

[The Poetess]

Polite Farewell

Cafe Transition Scene with The Professor
Edutainment Enlightens
Sexual Morality
Regulation 274
Media Brainwashing

OTHER CHARACTERS SONNETS

[The Storyteller]

[The Tourist]

Peer Pride!
English Second Language!
Intrusion Inquisition

[The Lovers]

Future Meeting	67 book 7
Kind Invitation	133 book 7
Love Gamble	20 book 3
Bare Necessities	32 book 3
Choice Or Convenience	173 book 7
Don Juan's Banana	184 book 7
Python In The Phaeton	81 book 3
Hairpin In A Haystack	38 book 5
A Few Drinks	173 book 6
Christmas Is Here (song)	151 book 5
Your Last Day	194 book 7
Life's Important Experiences	25 book 5

[The Leaders]
[The Queen]

The Queen's Glimpse	4 book 7
Royal Tea	37 book 1
Loyal Subjects	182 book 5
Immigration Bill	24 book 7
with The General three above	
Diatribe Of A Tribe	166 book 7
Let The Sun Shine	124 book 5

to The Guests

[The General]
Blood Red Fields
An American General   135 book 7
Gateway For Infidels   173 book 5
Key To His Heart   141 book 7
Ice Age Is Over   123 book 5
    with The Queen four above

[The Lawyer]
Whims Of A Judge   179 book 5
    with The Prostitute vs The Tourist
Chief Thief   140 book 6
    with The Trader
Stab In The Back   196 book 7
    with The Gossip
Jail or Bail?   43 book 5
Bill C-38 Civil Marriage Act
    with all the Characters above

[The ESL Students]
Amusing Accents   197 book 7
Measuring Monument   148 book 7
    Student 2

XXX RATED FULL VERSION ONLY

[The Chairman]

Complaints By Principle
Museum And Artifacts   150 book 7

[The Gossip]

Seven Sins   171 book 7
   with The Prostitute
Slut Or Prostitute   53 book 5
Chicken Gibbet   60 book 1
Stab In The Back   196 book 7
   with The Lawyer

[The Prostitute / The Maid]

Touring Locally   163 book 6
   with The Tourist
Poor Woman's Choices   163 book 7
Seven Sins   171 book 7
   with The Gossip
Smouldering Secrets   142 book 5
A Few Drinks   173 book 6
   with The Male of The Lovers

SONNET BOOK SERIES

For original versions of the sonnets in the stage play, refer to the series of sonnet books available in Lulu.com. Refer to http://www.lulu.com/spotlight/isarte

Some Differences Between Two Versions

Characters -- some are in or out, or in both

Costumes -- the Censored can show Characters wearing conservative attire but wild and revealing in the XXX version

Expressions -- even social behaviour, face and body mannerisms can change to show more sexual, transgender, gay in XXX, more emotional and exaggerated

Actions -- moving and placement of the Performers, entrances and exits, positions and body language, flow of the story from one scene to another can be more loud and exaggerated, more physical, or more wild random in the full XXX

Voices -- tone, volume, cadence, tempo, can be more temperamental and histrionic in the full XXX

Sets and Scenes – images chosen for projections and facades built can be more colourful and garish, obscene, gaudy, etc. in the full XXX

PROSE + POETRY = PROSETRY

The sonnet poems can be read either as poetry or prose. Poetic emphasizes the end rhyming sounds of the poetic lines and the non-practical, while prosaic the meaning of words and the practical.

Modern Sonnet Poems

A hybrid version with fourteen poetic lines and ten syllables per line compose the style and the rhyme scheme alternating ababcdcdefef with a couplet gg at the end.

Focus on Poetic

Example: The Loquacious Lecturer.
<u>Professor:</u> Thinking my purpose is to en<u>lighten</u>   (a)
Your minds, I, Professor Wroth speak <u>lectures</u>   (b)
With intelligence, hoping to <u>lighten</u>   (a)
Your darkness. All doubts and blind conj<u>ectures</u>   (b)
Shall be discarded just like igno<u>rance</u>. (c)
I shall explain everything. All ques<u>tions</u> (d)
Answered correctly, contrite tempe<u>rance</u> (c)
In check. Unrealistic expecta<u>tions</u>   (d)

Of your parents will thus be ex<u>ceeded</u>. (e)
You will walk out of here truly kn<u>owing</u> (f)
The English language.
<u>Storyteller:</u> He then ac<u>ceded</u>   (e)
Their limitations.
<u>Professor:</u> You will be <u>owing</u>   (f)
Me your mental development. Impl<u>ore</u> (g)
Gods, 'homo loquax et in hoc temp<u>ore</u>'! (g)

Focus on Prosaic

<u>Professor:</u> Thinking my purpose is to
enlighten your minds, I, Professor Wroth
speak lectures with intelligence, hoping to
lighten your darkness. All doubts and blind
conjectures shall be discarded just like
ignorance. I shall explain everything. All
questions answered correctly, contrite
temperance in check. Unrealistic
expectations of your parents will thus be
exceeded. You will walk out of here truly
knowing the English language.
<u>Storyteller:</u> He then acceded their
limitations.
<u>Professor:</u> You will be owing me your
mental development. Implore gods, 'homo
loquax et in hoc tempore'!

Readings

When reading the poetic play, The Character underlined with a colon symbol is supposed to read the line to the right of it. The sonnet titles are read usually either by The Professor or The Storyteller, except for the XXX Characters. Some of the sonnets are divided by lines with two or more Characters taking turns reading or some sonnets are read only by one Character. The notes are not read, ditto anything in brackets or parentheses, nor instructions for stage and screen, nor part sections.

Stage Sets and Screens

Stage has 3 parts: fixed center classroom in main level with a Teachers Lounge above it, left Red Light District with bench and street lamp, back may be a painted wood facade with cut out windows and platform behind for dancers; right movable Mini Sets for The Characters on floor platform with wheels.

Screens: behind the mini set on the right, sometimes if using screen projection changes depending on sonnet or fixed painted wood background.

The Professor's Lessons Stage
Full XXX Rated Version

ESL Class Room in Center

Movable Mini Set on Right

Red Light District on Left

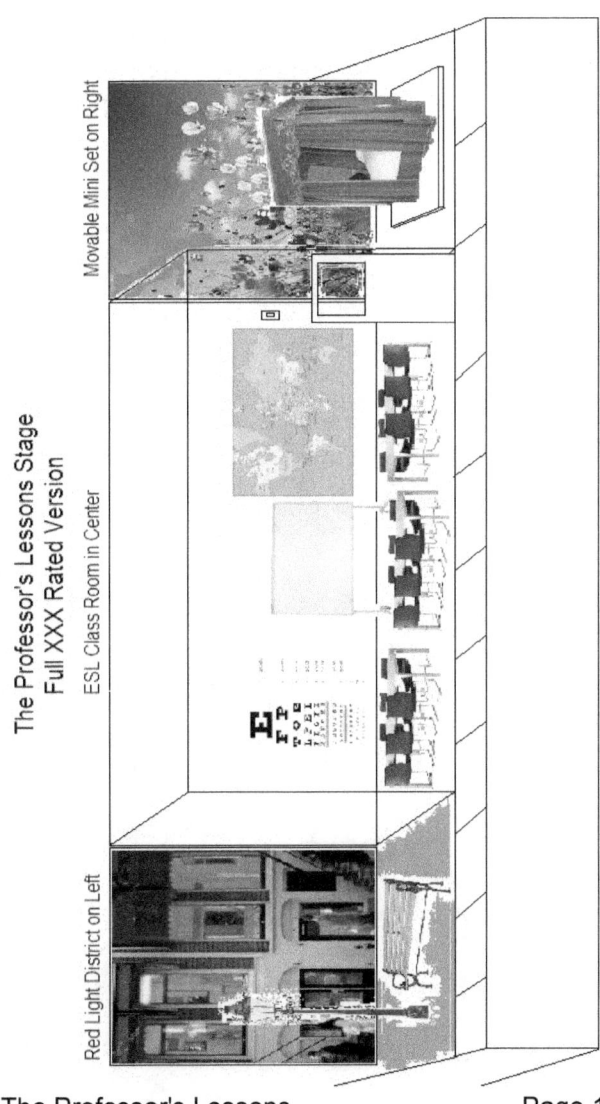

The Professor's Lessons

The Professor's Lessons Stage
Censored Version

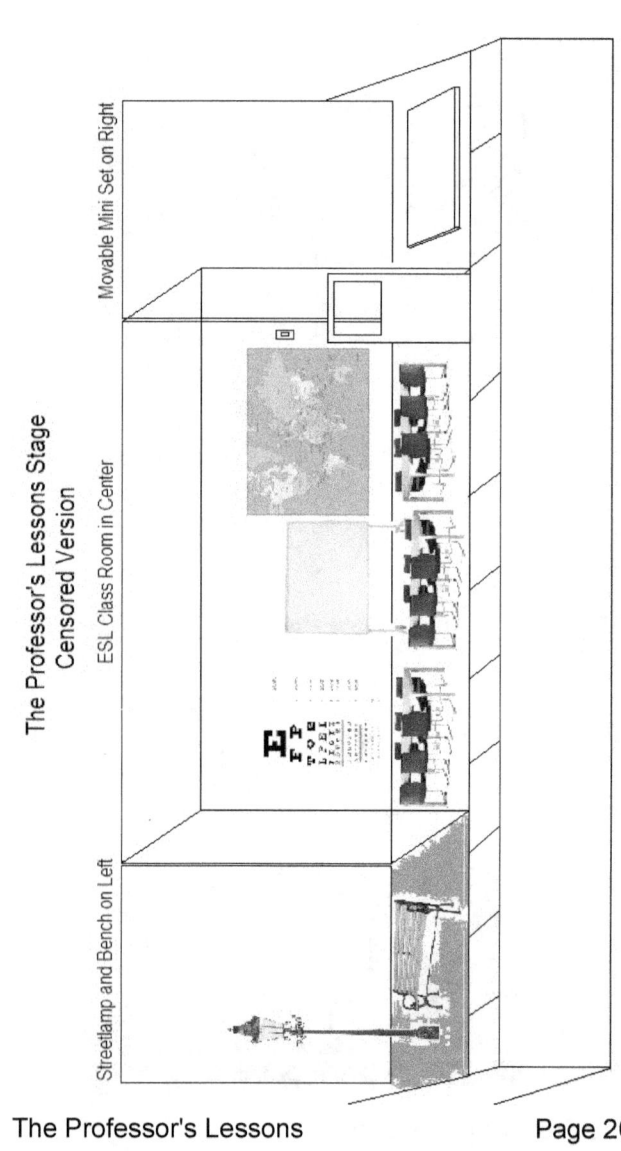

Streetlamp and Bench on Left

ESL Class Room in Center

Movable Mini Set on Right

OPENING

Stage: three part stage with Center Class Room with table and chairs, white board, world map, reading eye chart

Note: Storyteller can read unseen off stage, or be a recording, or can be a performer dressed in eccentric or conventional costume and wander around theater audience with a small spotlight with a wireless mic throughout the play, depending on production and direction. Twenty students gradually enter the center class room and take their seats.

<u>The Storyteller:</u> The Professor's Lessons
Being worldly, filled with erudi<u>tion</u>,
Professor Helmut Wroth, with a M<u>aster</u>
Of Communication, perfect dic<u>tion</u>,
Teaches English, although his thoughts
f<u>aster</u>
Than his foreign students wroth confu<u>sion</u>!
Language was his forte, but Metaphys<u>ics</u>
Influence on Earth's civiliza<u>tion</u>,
Plus the occult and spiritual psych<u>ics</u>
Gained him the reputation -- Ec<u>centric</u>
Egocentric! His wisdom from lost pl<u>anes</u>
Of existence, various ethno<u>centric</u>

Groups, foreign travels, including al<u>iens</u>
And invisible beings, obl<u>ivious</u>
To others, were to him very ob<u>vious</u>!

<u>Professor:</u> Class why is it dark in here? Let there be light!

Note: The Professor magically appears with smoke, flicks on light switch, timed with lightning bolt effect with thunder sound.
Credit FreeSFX Thunder
http://www.freesfx.co.uk/rx2/mp3s/1/941_1245800589.mp3

<u>Professor:</u> Good afternoon class!

<u>ESL Students:</u> Good afternoon, Professor Helmut Wroth!

<u>Professor:</u> I will take attendance. Say Present and Raise your hand if you are here.

Note: He names twenty students. ex. Lei, Mario

<u>Students:</u> Present (after name called).

PART ONE
Language Lessons

<u>Storyteller:</u> Part One: The Language Lessons.

This English as a Second Language class is taught by Professor Helmut Wroth, with a Master's Degree in Communication. He does educational lectures in international schools and is quite

The Loquacious Lecturer.

<u>Professor:</u> Thinking my purpose is to en<u>lighten</u>
Your minds, I, Professor Wroth speak <u>lectures</u>
With intelligence, hoping to <u>lighten</u>
Your darkness. All doubts and blind conj<u>ectures</u>
Shall be discarded just like igno<u>rance</u>.
I shall explain everything. All ques<u>tions</u>
Answered correctly, contrite tempe<u>rance</u>
In check. Unrealistic expecta<u>tions</u>
Of your parents will thus be ex<u>ceeded</u>.
You will walk out of here truly kn<u>owing</u>
The English language.

Storyteller: He then acceded
Their limitations.
Professor: You will be owing
Me your mental development. Implore
Gods, 'homo loquax et in hoc tempore'!

Storyteller: Being popular with foreign
students and the general public gained him
a reputation for having an eccentric style
of erudition with his

Lectures And Listeners.
Professor: Knowing Fate's strength I warn,
a futility
Of Will against Society. Its textures
And tides, will need swimmers ability
For survival. Swim or sink! My lectures
Teach students that language decides
careers.
After graduation, your lives edited
By employers and business. In arrears,
Whether successful or failed, credited
To all teachers are your minds.
Storyteller: Influential,
He exuded conceit from European
Intellect.

Professor: An idea, influenzal
Virus affects listeners. A paean
For spreading what we all internalize,
The skills to read, write, speak and analyze.

Professor: I will educate you today in some
language lessons followed by Character
lessons, introducing them and how they use
English in their occupations. Also
announcing, a new school competition for
longest words used --

Note: He reads it from a page to The Students.

The Sesquipedalian Award.
Professor: 'Considering students who pay
tuition,
Propensity for polysyllabic
Words shall be awarded. Institution
Grants to the teacher. Latin, Arabic,
Not included in the dictionary,
Do not count.' Announcing competition
Rules to the school caused reactionary
Resistance. Should we start a petition
With foreign students? Popularity
Votes by students, not administration,

Just learning English, needing clarity...
Storyteller: Immigrant students sensed his frustration.
Professor: 'Chiaroscuro' or 'ignominy'
Were submitted to decide nominee.

Student 1 Mario: Ig...no...miny?
Ig...no...miny?

Professor: Ignominy is the feeling of deep personal embarrassment and disgrace.

Student 1: Embarrass...ment and disgrace?

Storyteller: One foreign student seemed to be having difficulty pronouncing polysyllabic words resulting in

Scrabbler's Obfuscation.
Professor: Pondering on a grammar fumble rule
To explain a new student's stuttering,
I Wroth, have warned all, chattering cruel
Words in class should be in low muttering.
Others laugh. A newcomer's bemusement
Pronouncing complex English with diction

Cause a complex for this crowd's
a<u>musement</u>.
<u>Student 1:</u> I play Scrabble.
<u>Professor:</u> Your teacher's pre<u>diction</u> --
Let me guess. You research words by
<u>Google</u>.
Written words understood, but your ac<u>cent</u>
Verbalized boggles! Error rate, <u>googol</u>
Ratio of success, bet dollar to <u>cent</u>...
My advice is eschew obfus<u>cation</u>.
Simple words 'chewing' not 'mast<u>ication</u>'!

<u>Professor:</u> Instead of feeling
embarrassment, you can avoid the shame
of mispronouncing complex words by using
their simple equivalents. Even if you play
Scrabble and are an expert in the written
word, to pronounce words correctly you
have to practise from simple to complex
polysyllabic words.

Note: Then from the audience, a student loudly
sings. Two other strangers repeat it in agreement.

<u>The Heckler:</u> 'It's rotten in Denmark' --
spoiled milk curdles!

<u>Student 1:</u> (stands and looks around)

Note: Student 1 stands and looks towards the back of the class audience, ditto The Professor.

<u>Storyteller:</u> Disturbed by the interruption of The Professor's advice to a student, they all look towards the back of the class audience to see who it was. They both felt bothered by a stranger's heckling, feeling a

Stigma From An Enigma.
<u>Student 1:</u> Should I ignore any racial in<u>sult</u>?
<u>Professor:</u> In public?

Credit Free SFX Male Laugh
http://www.freesfx.co.uk/rx2/mp3s/4/4713_13313026 04.mp3

<u>Student 1:</u> Why do you laugh in per<u>verse</u> Humour.?
<u>Professor:</u> Take insults with a grain of <u>salt</u>! Not everyone likes foreign rhyming <u>verse</u>.
<u>Student 1:</u> It is English, a public <u>oration</u> With a loud heckler willing to de<u>vote</u> Effort against our collab<u>oration</u>.

Professor: Who expects the popularity <u>vote</u>
Without education, fame nor for<u>tune</u>?
Student 1: It is embarrassing. All these
hu<u>rdles</u>
To success...
Professor: He was chanting out of <u>tune</u>.
'It's rotten in Denmark -- spoiled milk
cu<u>rdles</u>!'
Student 1: Who is it for? Who was that
tor<u>mentor</u>?
Storyteller: They puzzled for whom --
student or <u>mentor</u>?

Storyteller: The Professor then knew there
was a crowd reaction and speculated a
possible hidden communication via

Racial Telepathy.
Professor: Whatever thought enters the
head of <u>one</u>
Enters all of them instanta<u>neously</u>!
The whole crowd murmurs disturbed.
Every<u>one</u>
Gets upset! Thus beliefs erro<u>neously</u>
Are transmitted within the same ra<u>cial</u>
Group, but outsiders are indif<u>ferent</u>,

Not being affected.

Student 1: Is this special
Ability per person, coherent
Only in matters pertaining to race?

Storyteller: Professor Wroth nodded.

Professor: Fortunately
So. Racial telepathy based on face,
Skin, eyes, nose and genome map, innately
Broadcasts shared thoughts and feelings
without words
To each group, protecting with pens or
swords.

Professor: Class, time to return to our
language lessons.

Storyteller: The Professor then related how
without education, people can remain

Modern Savages.

Professor: Ignorance can breed modern
savages
Uncivilized in primitive instincts:
Hunger, shelter, mating through ravages
On land. Lack of territorial precincts,
Such brutes roam under laws of the jungle.

But without protection from such d<u>anger</u>,
Cultured civilians would fear to b<u>ungle</u>
Their wild campaigns, as thwarting may
<u>anger</u>
Them. My solution is to edu<u>cate</u>,
Thus taming pagans violent ex<u>pression</u>.
All my lectures and career dedi<u>cate</u>
Towards civilizing by sup<u>pression</u>,
Organizing societies: Philist<u>ines</u>,
Vandals, Barbarians, tribes from
Philipp<u>ines</u>...

<u>Professor:</u> If there are no laws but many
freedoms following people's primitive
instincts for necessities: food, shelter, sex,
then people might remain savages in a
modern world. Any questions?

<u>Poetess (unseen voice):</u> Which primitive
instinct remains a compulsion for you, dear
Professor Wroth? Food, shelter, or sex?

Note: Professor Wroth looks around puzzled,
wondering where her voice is coming from.

<u>Professor:</u> Class? Do you hear any other

voice talking in our classroom? I am not
sure if I am only imagining it.

Storyteller: His class denies hearing
anyone else talking, so he proceeds to
contrast primitive societies with modern

        Canadian Civilization.
Professor: Immigrants gather from various
ethnic
Backgrounds to join a multicultural
Celebration, expressing the technique
Of tolerance for horticultural
Flower gardens, colourful and diverse.
Citizenship in this global village,
The human species in this universe,
Means forgiving historical pillage
For museums, love of diversity
In humanity. To join this loud crowd,
Learn world cultures in university.
Listen politely as talking aloud
In public leads to mute segregation,
But those civilized reach integration.

Professor: Modern civilization versus
uncivilized primitive has laws to curb

people's instincts and freedoms. Diversity is through approved immigration not invasion and requires respect and tolerance.

Storyteller: His students knew their own foreign languages from other countries, but in learning English, this sometimes resulted in

Confused Translations.
Professor: If all languages in your heads confused
You when translating lines...grammar, spelling,
Meaning, accent, stress can all be infused
With misunderstanding when retelling
From one foreign language to another.
My quick students learn by conversation,
Reading and writing. No need to bother
With literal word by word translation.
It can be confusing, but persevere
With other foreigners also struggling.
Please follow my advice. It is severe,
But meaning matters more than word juggling.

Thus, no longer use a dictio<u>nary</u>,
Thesaurus, choosing the ord<u>inary</u>.

<u>Professor:</u> When learning English, just
think, speak, read, write in English without
translating to your other languages. It is
easier to learn a language on its own.

<u>Storyteller:</u> Observant, The Professor
noticed both the obvious and the oblivious
attention from students in his class. He
worried whether they were listening or had

A Finger In Each Ear.
<u>Professor:</u> As your teacher, giving class
<u>instruction</u>
Is a pleasure that I could edu<u>cate</u>
You in grammar and sentence co<u>nstruction</u>.
Class, use language with meaning,
dedi<u>cate</u>
Your dialogue to explain.
<u>Storyteller:</u> On white <u>board</u>,
He took a pen and asked his favour<u>ite</u>
Student (despite the ESL School <u>Board</u>
Advice)
<u>Professor:</u> Lei, please compose a line of

wi<u>t</u>.

<u>Student 2 Lei:</u> Professor, watching you makes me <u>listen</u>.

<u>Storyteller:</u> The class laughed.

<u>Professor:</u> The target missed by <u>missile</u>! You pouted. (Note: said to her or use "She pouted." or "Who doubted?" if to the class)

<u>Student 2:</u> Your eyes twinkle, lips <u>glisten</u>...

<u>Professor:</u> Dear, your compliments can mean dis<u>missal</u>!

<u>Student 2:</u> When words are said, a finger in each <u>ear</u>,

What twit is heard or understood...far, n<u>ear</u>?

<u>Professor:</u> Class please watch, listen, to me and pay full attention!

<u>Storyteller:</u> The Professor tried to regain control of his class and continue with a lesson in

Punctuating Sentences.

<u>Professor:</u> Ending sentences with these marks: ques<u>tion</u>

Asks an answer, answer with a peri<u>od</u>,

Command or surprise with exclama<u>tion</u>.

In conversations about subjects, fo<u>od</u>

For thought, when in doubt, hang by ellips<u>is</u>.

<u>Student 2:</u> Sir, how do we all learn to pronunci<u>ate</u>?

<u>Storyteller:</u> Professor Wroth glanced at the girl whose lips k<u>iss</u>

In dreams, with a full mouth as if she <u>ate</u>

Honey...

<u>Student 2:</u> Sir, we all have foreign ac<u>cents</u>!

<u>Professor:</u> Practise at home.

<u>Storyteller:</u> Using his sweetest <u>tone</u>,

He imagined sniffing her perfumed s<u>cents</u>

And suggested,

<u>Professor:</u> Call me on teleph<u>one</u>!

I can teach you every <u>grammatical</u>

Rule; use for living and d<u>ramatical</u>.

The Professor's Lessons   Page 36

Storyteller: Professor Wroth enthused further about using punctuation for emotion and tried to warn them about losing a stream of consciousness while thinking and talking simultaneously in a

Comatose Comma.

Professor: Ending each sentence with punctuation
Marks, you can stress your skills in linguistics.
Emotional? Do use exclamation,
Raising your voice at the end, semantics
Notwithstanding, every other sentence.
Extroverted? Do converse in parties
For hours on end, not sitting on the fence,
By taking one stance only, if you please.
Do ask questions and please end your statements
With suitable expressions, inflections,
Including facial and body movements
For emphasis. Bacterial infections
Can attack throat and brain. In a comma
Pause in a sentence, avoid a coma!

Storyteller: He tried to focus on teaching

his entire class, but from the moment she walked in, The Professor felt Lei would become his favourite foreign student and she did sometimes cause his subconscious thoughts to wonder and wander from his stream of consciousness. Love walked in the door and would influence his

Language Lessons.

Professor: Knowing language by its repetition
You can write simple phrases per language.
Practise daily like in competition
To win. Pronunciation and accent gauge
Intellect.

Storyteller: The class adored their teacher.
His favourite girl student could amuse
Him by her ignorance.

Note: The next sentences can be a recording offstage for The Professor's thoughts in his voice. He can be writing on the board and sometimes looking at her.

Professor (recorded thoughts): I can teach her
To say anything! To choose her as muse,

All romantic languages: Ita<u>lian</u>,
Spanish, French, English, with their
col<u>loquial</u>
Lines from common to royal Casti<u>lian</u>
And Latin, till she sounds like a <u>local</u>.
Her lips and voice would give words their
<u>meaning</u>
Of love! But if cold, make them
de<u>meaning</u>...

<u>Storyteller:</u> The Professor wrote simple
phrases on the white board:
I love you.
You are beautiful and I am handsome.
We are both intelligent.
Will you marry me?

<u>Professor:</u> Class, please repeat these
simple phrases after me to practise
pronunciation.
I love you.
You are beautiful and I am handsome.
We are both intelligent.
Will you marry me?

<u>Students together:</u> I love you.

You are beautiful and I am handsome.
We are both intelligent.
Will you marry me?

PART TWO
The Characters

<u>Storyteller:</u> Part Two: Introduction of The
Major Characters.
The Professor, being also a Master of
Metaphysics can enter other planes of
existence. He is omniscient and aware
of the fictional Characters and makes his
class aware of them when needed, but they
are not aware of him and his class.

Note: Through lighting, focus awareness from the
class, then dim it to light the Major Characters
instead, then shadow the class.

<u>Professor:</u> Okay, now class it is time to
move on to the next section. I will introduce
fictional Characters who will demonstrate
more lessons using language for effective
communication in their roles in life. With
my metaphysical powers, I will allow you all
to see through the class room walls on the

side to see the fictional Characters as they relate their experiences.

<u>Poetess (unseen voice):</u> We are all Characters in reality and fiction. Some of us know who we are and the roles we play in life but some remain unaware and lost...

[The Teacher]

<u>Professor:</u> The Teacher -- let us start with The Teacher, myself. As I have said at the beginning, I am here to instruct you, the foreign adult students to learn English for whatever reasons you have chosen to be here and learn from my teaching! This is about a language teacher from the musical My Fair Lady, based on the play Pygmalion, the

Perfect Professor.
<u>Professor:</u> Mastering English speech by phone<u>tics</u>,
Professor Higgins, wealthy bache<u>lor</u>
And expert in social dialec<u>tics</u>,
Observed class distinctions from poor

squa<u>lor</u>
To clean lavishness. No Cinde<u>rella</u>
In his life until Eliza, lips <u>pursed</u>
Enters. He supports her, an umb<u>rella</u>,
To teach her a class where a man's slip<u>pers</u>
Show wealth, from house, speech,
breeding, to his sh<u>oe</u>.
Correct pronunciation of 'rain in S<u>pain</u>',
Plus 'h' and vowels 'a, e, i, o, <u>u</u>',
Could uplift one in Society. The <u>pain</u>
Of learning language, no matter how <u>late</u>,
Was rewarded with clothes and choco<u>late</u>...

<u>Storyteller:</u> A floating box of chocolate
enters the room as he extends his hand
towards it. He then walks to Lei and offers
her a piece, then hands it to his Students.

<u>Professor:</u> Here, have a chocolate.

Floating Chocolate Box

Classic Chocolates

*The pain
Of learning language, no matter how late,
Was rewarded with clothes and chocolate...*

[The Tourist]

Overhead Screen in Classroom: Polynesia moai statues of Easter Island

<u>Professor</u>: Now for the first Character, The Tourist. Just like Captain James Cook, a British explorer, who was a pioneer tourist and discovered a primitive island culture on Easter Island also known as Rapa Nui and how he was mistaken for their god Lono. Cook also realized unfortunately what usually goes together are

Taboos & Travels.

<u>Professor</u>: Captain Cook saw Polynesian <u>Eden</u>,
Rapa Nui known as Easter Is<u>land</u>,
With moai statues guarding forb<u>idden</u>
Trespassers. With ship and crew, they did <u>land</u>
Befriending the native chiefs, priests and <u>tribes</u>.
Certain customs as cannib<u>alism</u>
And sex orgies were tapu, but with b<u>ribes</u>
Could be indulged in. Coloni<u>alism</u>

Changed their society with Christianity
And foreign marriages with Europeans.
Underneath the mixing, the vanity
Of being a white god with brown peons,
Along with trading, compelled explorers
To far shores to enter as visitors.

Professor: Refer to encyclopedias or online Wikipedia and The Project Gutenberg EBook of Captain Cook's Journal for further reading.
Refer to: http://www.gutenberg.org/files/8811/8811-index.htm

Poetess (unseen voice): Mistaken for a god? Hmm... Professor Wroth maybe you might have the same problem with foreign students?

Back Screen of Mini Set: Island beach scene with coconut trees

Note: The Tourist enters the mini set.

Professor: So here is The Tourist, who will show how language is used for travel and tourism to welcome foreigners in

Island Hospitality.

Tourist: Born in this tropical monsoon island

Sheltered by banana, coconut trees,

This Earth's Paradise is mine! I demand.

In God's Church, I will pray with rosaries

That each typhoon, quake, eruption and storm

Shall cease immediately. All coloured fish,

Natives, foreigners, tourists shall conform

To tribal laws. If offered a home dish --

Roast pig, blood stew -- in camaraderie

Everyone must feast to avoid world wars.

Let this modern jungle be sanctuary;

We'll display hospitality in bars.

Entertain yourselves in our cheap burlesque;

Have fun, relax! It is so picturesque!

Back Screen of Mini Set: Diversity and Immigration photo

Professor: There is a growing global trend towards internationalization via immigration and tourism. If tourists become immigrants and come in legally approved by

authorities, they can join the diversity of
Canada and United States of America
choosing

Mosaic Versus Melting Pot.
<u>Tourist:</u> Multiculturalism acce<u>pted</u>
Foreign ethnic influences brought <u>by</u>
Immigrants, who were poor and indeb<u>ted</u>
To the wealthier countries who could <u>buy</u>
Their humility. Of course, I'm grate<u>ful</u>
To the First World and their techn<u>ology</u>:
Cars, computers, television. A <u>fool</u>
Would ignore progress for ec<u>ology</u>
And conservation. To argue fur<u>ther</u>.
The U.S.A.'s melting pot, Can<u>ada's</u>
Mosaic are enriched by cultures o<u>ther</u>
Than mainstream. Things like pina col<u>adas</u>,
Coffee, bananas, bagels, im<u>ported</u>
In, count. Why would aliens be de<u>ported</u>?

*Back Screen of Mini Set: Canada border
with cars*

<u>Professor:</u> Tourists learn a common
language such as English to open doors of
opportunities in countries that use that

language. English is the most international and worldly language, with a lot of foreign allusions and inclusions, making it a useful, worldly

Common Language.
<u>Tourist:</u> Understanding cultures, multilin<u>gual</u>
Travellers easily entered na<u>tions</u>.
Doors opened for educated, eq<u>ual</u>
To locals' skill levels. Nobody <u>shuns</u>
Us translators who can commun<u>icate</u>
In their mother tongues. Written and ver<u>bal</u>
Words are master keys used to ded<u>icate</u>
Smart bridges between cultural, tri<u>bal</u>,
Historical differences. Coun<u>tries</u>
That share a common language are
peace<u>ful</u>.
If we view the entire forest for <u>trees</u>
As a lingual group, not one is a <u>fool</u>.
Border officials passed my inter<u>view</u>,
Six months temporary until re<u>view</u>.

Back Screen of Mini Set: bus on street

<u>Professor:</u> Getting to know Canada, a

tourist can be lost, needing the help of a
friendly local to show him around town, as
he tries

Touring Locally.
Tourist: With camcorder handy, I ride public
Transit pretending as an immigrant.
Urban cityscapes are not bucolic
Countrysides, I wander as a vagrant
Exploring. I speak with a passenger.
Prostitute: I was born here so I know this
city
And locals. Are you a new messenger
Delivering something? I do pity
You seem lost and new.
Tourist: Really, how can you
Tell?
Prostitute: Not sure, but carrying a bus
map,
Camera, backpack can mean someone
new.
Tourist: I am curious and need to fill a gap
Until I know.
Prostitute: Do avoid loitering
In suburbs and refrain from littering.

Note: They walk away together and exit stage.

Professor: So there goes The Tourist, a foreigner who learned to speak English to travel and to immigrate, accompanied by a Local who can probably practise English with him and show him around town!
Since you are foreign students here, you are also tourists and you can use the language skills learned in my class to do the same, tour and explore the city.

Storyteller: To lighten his foreign students mood, considering that in some countries non-citizen foreigners are labelled aliens, The Professor recalled that in the past on some subjects, he was a

Self-Taught Lecturer.

Professor: Lecturing on subjects I barely knew,
As professor I admit, I'm self-taught!
Whatever came to my mind, old or new
Info would be shared. No one yet has caught
Me in error. The audience applauded
Amused. I was lecturing on spaceships.

Any object entering explo<u>ded</u>
From impact, till anti-gravity sl<u>ips</u>
Into the earth atmosphere en<u>abled</u>
Their entry. The crowd believed my lo<u>gic</u>!
<u>Student 2:</u> Did any aliens end up dis<u>abled</u>?
<u>Professor:</u> People laughed. Yes in Roswell,
a tra<u>gic</u>
Crash where an alien with intel<u>ligence</u>
Was scrutinized with man's due di<u>ligence</u>.

[The Broadcaster]

*Mini Set: tv studio with tv camera on
tripod, mic, focus light on tripod wheels,
large tv monitor with recorded videos or use
back screen to project some image relevant
to the sonnets*

*Back Screen of Mini Set: Media logo, time
zone map, same for all reports*

Note: The Professor can do the intro sonnet in the
mini tv studio set.

*TV Monitor: video of dead media covered
by banana leaves*

Professor: The second Character, The Broadcaster broadcasts thru radio, television and computers, news worthy of public attention such as: weather, politics, economy, and crime. It is currently a dangerous occupation in some countries with political corruption of power to suppress the freedom of expression of media. Insecure, the media realize they will cover

No More Power.

Professor: Analyzing the media mass*acre*,
They realized the danger of p*ower*!
Their colleagues lie buried under *acre*.
Perhaps for fear of death, they should c*ower*
From Government? What if critic*ism*
Results in suits of libel and sl*ander*
Or worse murder? They agreed a sch*ism*
Divided authority. To p*ander*
For their approval, stating *compliments*
In print, radio, tv and inter*net*
Broadcasting to the public, *complements*
Their popular goals – catch more fish by *net*!

Let them report about comm<u>unity</u>,
Not politicians with imp<u>unity</u>!

<u>Professor:</u> Refer to Wikipedia and the
Committee to Project Journalists CPJ for
the 'the single deadliest event for journalists
in history' in the Philippines!
Refer to:
<u>http://en.wikipedia.org/wiki/2009_Philippines_massa</u>
<u>cre</u>

TV Monitor: video of Syrian war coverage
Note: The Broadcaster enters set and sits in the
studio.

<u>Professor:</u> Currently, in Syria according to
media, the civil war between rebel soldiers
and army soldiers continues displacing the
people as refugees to nearby countries
assisted by the United Nations. Media
report wars around the world and here is
the Broadcaster's report following the trend
of Arab Spring, a

Village Rebellion!
<u>Broadcaster:</u> News in Canada read 'Mi<u>litary</u>
Echelon of Syria killed' to fr<u>ighten</u>

Their government towards solitary
Resignation. UN plans, to tighten
By economic sanctions for a peace
Plan and ceasefire with rebels, were
thwarted.
Violence and murders were used to release
Currents, which Egypt uprisings started.
Forty years in political power
With their own military protection.
Looking down from an ivory tower
To kill villagers after election.
People take arms to join the rebellion,
Fighting their government's war battalion!

TV Monitor: video of veterans wheelchairs

Professor: Reports continue about war
heroes showing one of the unfortunate
tragic after effects of the price of war --
disabilities of veterans who after a war
overseas become

Vainglorious Victims.
Broadcaster: Wars are fought over vast
territories,
Natural resources, great principles,

Protecting themselves, allies. Victories
Are won by strength, strategy and peoples,
Led by their long-term goals, God's grace,
vision,
And global greed. With determination,
Success is attained! The television
Blared the news of final termination
Of the lengthy oil wars fought overseas.
The tired seniors maneuver their
wheelchairs.
Some were veterans whose lives were on
lease
By God's mercy. With their legs lost, who
cares
About them? Their blood shed in
vainglorious
Wars. Their sole comfort, we are victorious!

TV Monitor: video of subway train damage in UK

<u>Professor:</u> After terror incidents in public places, such as the Twin Towers in the USA and subway bombing in the United Kingdom, the media coverage alarmed governments globally, to question

foreigners and determine whether they are

Tourists Or Terrorists?

Broadcaster: It happened without warning
– the subway
Stations were bombed. The United
Kingdom
Press covered news. Every dog has its day.
Minority immigrant groups had come
To shake international relations
With bombs. Police became more vigilant
At entrances and exits. All nations
Must be in red flag alert! Now recant
Former policies of anonymous
Travelling without tight security
Checking identification. Famous
Or not, please ask for identity.
Perhaps then, they can weed the terrorists
From the crowds full of innocent tourists.

*TV Monitor: video of red light district of
Amsterdam with The Prostitute*

Note: At right Mini Set the tv screen of The
Broadcaster can show the Red Light District where
at left side, under a red lamp and bench, The

Prostitute is walking and posing around, waiting to pick up a customer until the end of the next sonnet. At center the darkened class room with Professor.

Professor: Some media report on profitable corrupting businesses such as brothels, casinos, bars, strip clubs, pornography including alcohol and cigarettes, which in a designated red light district such as in Amsterdam Netherlands, governments can charge taxes under an umbrella

Sin Tax.

Broadcaster: Government worried that the deficit
In the budget meant cuts in services
Or raises in taxes. The illicit
Activities, the corrupting vices:
Smoking, drinking, and soon prostitution
Were discussed as potential taxable
Goods and services. Should Constitution
Change so these penalties build a stable
Economy? How much in revenue
Will be earned in taxing the cigarettes,
Alcohol, and whores in each avenue?
They calculated, adding gambling bets

In casinos. They call it the 'Sin Tax'
To profit from sinners through Law's syntax.

Storyteller: Off the air, as the tv crew pack
up their equipment, they joke around with

The Eloquent Broadcaster.
Technician 1: Silent Sam? Recall with
embarrassment
How his gastroenteritis caused him
Discomfort...
Broadcaster: My coworkers harassment
Is infuriating! It's not me. Blame Kim!
Let's point my finger at her... She denied
It. Must we talk about this for hours?
Technician 1: But it smelled like a spring
roll.
Technician 2 Kim: My quick snide
Retort. Or a garden full of flowers!
Broadcaster: What are you talking about?
Hot air!
Why are you all blaming me? Not a sound
Heard. I'm so indignant. It is not fair,
After announcing the news to astound
Viewers about such sinners, flatulence
Is pardonable with such eloquence!

Note: Back in the classroom, although the Red Light District remains lighted with a red lamp during the conversation of The Prostitute and The Gossip.

<u>Professor:</u> So there goes The Broadcaster, reporting to the public on various international news topics from wars to vices.

[The Prostitute]

<u>Storyteller:</u> The Professor returns to class, continuing with the lessons by writing down the list of all The Characters he will introduce to them. While outside in the Red Light district, The Prostitute Maid ponders on a

Poor Woman's Choices.
<u>Prostitute:</u> Let me ponder what is best –
housek<u>eeping</u>
In rich houses or street pro<u>stitution</u>
For me as a lifestyle? What if sl<u>eeping</u>
With men gives escape from de<u>stitution</u>,
Enough for expenses from mascul<u>ine</u>
Generosity? Or would my reg<u>rets</u>
In losing morals make the femin<u>ine</u>

Option better, despite potential threats
Of being scolded and silenced? Choices
Of such employment have both defeating
And degrading effects! Mental voices
In my tired head leave me angry, seething
About my dilemma. Will my conceit
Or humility, be full of deceit?

Storyteller: The Gossip passes by and
gossips with The Prostitute about

Seven Sins.
Prostitute: Alas, I have felt all these seven
sins:
Wrath, greed, sloth, pride, gluttony, envy,
lust.
Gossip: Really? Have you experienced any
since
Yesterday?
Prostitute: I'm sure, I have. Could I trust
My vices with you? I envied women
With wealth, so my pride to be their equal
Cost a lot in jewellery. Their men
Were handsome, so I lusted for them while
Plotting how to hook them to be their slut.
Gossip: I'm amazed, how did you seduce

husbands?
Prostitute: My greed was to be supported in
sloth.
Our gluttony for food and wine in lands
Libidinous, our mutual temptation,
Tempered by self-wrath and contemplation.

Note: The Prostitute and The Gossip sit close to
each other on the bench, sharing personal
confidential gossip with each other.

Prostitute: Smouldering Secrets...
Repression can disguise hidden passions.
Society frowns on immoral women.
Some cultures will influence the fashions
And the ladies control desires of men.
Animal mating instincts are stifled.
Laws are then passed by men to regulate
Our lusts. Prostitutes and whores are trifled
For wives. Marriages will then strangulate
The affairs to maintain stability.
Attraction initiates relationships
Supported by compatibility.
Monogamy will keep the rest. The ships
Dock at one port and sailors seek red lights.
But police will arrest our wild delights.

[The Gossip]

<u>Gossip:</u>   Slut Or Prostitute?
Sex is sometimes a pleasurable <u>act</u>.
For women who remain single, it <u>may</u>
Be for variety or money. A f<u>act</u>
Is it's an old profession. With dis<u>may</u>
Or not, most men according to re<u>search</u>
Think about sex more than women.
Fem<u>ales</u>
Likewise, are sluts or prostitutes and <u>search</u>
For such men. How mainstream society
f<u>ails</u>
To give it respec<u>tability</u>,
Thus promiscuity is der<u>ided</u>.
This does cause conflict in s<u>tability</u>
And attitude is often div<u>ided</u>.
Should it be lauded and then leg<u>alized</u>?
Or should our honour remain scand<u>alized</u>?

<u>Storyteller:</u> Done with sharing his written
notes on the white board, The Professor
gradually becomes aware of the two
women outside and overhears some of their
gossiping dialogue. He steps outside to
watch them. Being a gentleman, he

does not usually acknowledge the existence of such women of ill repute.

<u>Poetess (unseen voice):</u> Wicked women exist luring men to sexual sin and carnal knowledge turning boys into men. But these ones charge a price, Professor Wroth.

Note: The Professor steps outside to scold the two women outside gossiping. He sees them but they do not see him only sense his presence.

<u>Professor:</u>   Gossiping Women?
How to avoid such a tempting <u>evil</u>
Is a goal we accomplish with a fr<u>own</u>.
"She's your enemy!" Whispers the D<u>evil</u>,
"She scatters dangerous seeds to be s<u>own</u>."
Don't we all prefer blessed sol<u>itude</u>?
In mingling, people, our souls get d<u>irty</u>.
Let's heed this good advice in grat<u>itude</u>;
No one's clean and innocent past th<u>irty</u>.
Redemption and soul rebirth fall<u>acious</u>:
Holy water's tap, that crouton's a <u>fake</u>;
The wine is juice; one can't be loqu<u>acious</u>

While dear St. Joan is burning at the st<u>ake</u>!
Gossip, women, is but a c<u>atalyst</u>
To sin and sorrow, says this f<u>atalist</u>.

<u>Professor:</u> You are disturbing my class. If you could please leave and find another place to chat.

<u>Storyteller:</u> Although he is invisible to them, the two women are slightly disturbed by his unseen presence and leave. The Professor tries to regain his usual composure and enters his class room.

Note: The Prostitute and The Gossip leave the bench feeling uneasy and chilled by The Professor's invisible annoyed presence. They exit stage. He returns to his class room.

Gossiping Women

*One can't be loquacious
While dear St. Joan is burning at the stake!*

<u>Professor:</u> Okay class, let us read aloud The Characters. We will go over everyone on this list by the end of this class session, so please write this list in your notebooks!
The Tourist -- Travel;
The Broadcaster -- News;
The Trader -- Business;
The Lovers -- Relationships;
The Leader -- Power; and
The Lawyer -- Law and Order

<u>Storyteller:</u> Not all the students were reading aloud, so The Professor noticed their blank faces and

Dead Souls.

<u>Poetess (unseen voice only):</u> Professor Wroth, the living dead are listening to you or daydreaming about someone else.

Note: A floating Ouija board goes towards The Professor extending his hand for it.

<u>Professor:</u> I suspect students use autom<u>atic</u>

Writing while watching me lecture in class,
Tomorrow's assignment! In an attic,
Take a Ouija board. Spirit of the glass,
Is a game for channelling messages.
Lay out the letters of the alphabet.
Student 2: Sir, what if ghosts misspell
words and sages
Do not make sense?
Professor: I will wager a bet
That you will either show intelligence
Or become confused, full of ignorance.
If Next day, I observe dumb diligence.
Retaining blank stares as if in a trance...
Class, if the ghosts in a Ouija session
Are smarter, please allow their possession!

Storyteller: The class laughed!

Credit FreeSFX Class laugh
http://www.freesfx.co.uk/rx2/mp3s/4/4725_13313026
30.mp3

Storyteller: But were they really going to
take his advice seriously or not and pay
more attention to Professor Helmut Wroth,
Master of Metaphysics and Communication

and their teacher in English as a Second Language?

[The Trader]

Mini Set: led trading board with company index and numbers, graph chart, paper mache or wood cutout life size bear and bull for stock market, fir tree in a pot.
Back Screen: Photo 10 Stock Exchange

<u>Professor:</u> Now we will move on to the third Character, The Trader who deals in small to big business, trading products, services and information in world markets, both importing and exporting, creating global

Business Empires.
<u>Professor:</u> Industrialization for commerci<u>al</u>
Products has enabled mass p<u>roduction</u>
To feed World Markets. Internation<u>al</u>
Trade for these goods are an int<u>roduction</u>
To business cooperation, world p<u>eace</u>,
The global village marketing con<u>cept</u>.
Countries that progressed, where vicious
wars c<u>ease</u>,

Are busy manufacturing, except
Nuclear or fire arms. Some European
Kingdoms established schools and factories
In the world: Asia, America and
Africa. All developing countries
Profiting from this imperialism
Are by-products of colonialism!

Back Screen of Mini Set: pine forest
Note: The Trader enters the mini set.

Professor: Recalling his roots in starting an
international small business, a linguist
realizes his mastery of language can
influence people even foreigners to buy
trees, so he becomes a

Tree Trade Master.
Trader: Mastering a global foreign
language
Such as English to improve my country,
Bavaria, I decided to engage
Traders in business. Buy a Christmas tree!
Pine or fir are ever green when planted.
These come from a nursery in clay pots.
Let me explain why they appear stunted...

I discussed pricing with: Brits, Celts and Sc<u>ots</u>.
These are branded under 'Ever Smi<u>tten</u>',
Meaning to last forever just like l<u>ove</u>.
I sold the trees in multiples of <u>ten</u>,
Gaining popularity. Take a d<u>ove</u>
With a Tannenbaum tree. Its' pur<u>ity</u>
Will delight with a tree's fidel<u>ity</u>!

Back Screen of Mini Set: NYSE building

<u>Professor:</u> The Trader then recalls his decision to become a stock adviser in New York Stock Exchange NYSE, the world's largest stock exchange on 11 Wall Street,

Wall Street Market.
<u>Trader:</u> Hopping up and down as a wa<u>llaby</u>,
The stock market thrives. Any walla<u>roo</u>
Survives this haggling to a lu<u>llaby</u>
Determined by the strange loss or acc<u>rue</u>
Of interest. Tough brokers on Wall St<u>reet</u>
Make or break fortunes overnight! "Su<u>gar</u>
Daddies control this trade." A parak<u>eet</u>
Might chirp. Commodities are so vul<u>gar</u>,
Dividends must be paid to common st<u>ock</u>

Holders as well. When prices drop, foolish
Investors sell causing bearish amok,
Although it is cheaper to buy. Bullish
Rises are best for selling. Thus buy low,
Sell high! This is a tip from those who know.

Back Screen of Mini Set: NYSE trading
floor and Skype session in island

Professor: Sick from the stress of stock
trading, The Trader retired to an island and
informs his former co-workers via Skype
about his current lifestyle change and a

Tahitian Taboo.
Trader: Carving wood souvenirs, tinted
tattoo
On face, I moved to this tiny island
Tahiti to retire, mate with girls too
And enjoy the beaches.
Co Worker 1: What a dull, bland
Lifestyle you live!
Co Worker 2: The New York stock market
Misses you.
Trader: I chat with ex co-workers
On Skype. Stocks cannot be in a basket,

Like fish or eggs. The stress felt by bro<u>kers</u>
Buying and selling, whether bear or <u>bull</u>,
Caused my heart attack! It is forb<u>idden</u>
For my health. I was a vicious pit-<u>bull</u>.
Now, my old bark and bite can be h<u>idden</u>.
The only thrill I'm allowed – a t<u>aboo</u>
Watching a nude girl in a peek-<u>a-boo</u>!

<u>Professor:</u> Trading can obviously be a
stressful occupation so retiring to an island
can be a big break! Class, it is time for a
brief recess break. Take ten minutes and
our lessons will continue after with the rest
of The Characters.

The Afternoon Break
Scene: Primitivism Party

<u>Storyteller:</u>   The Afternoon Break.
Professor Wroth steps outside and leaves
the class room to go to the Teachers
Lounge upstairs. Some students get up
and socialize with others, one student turns
on a boom box and plays ethnic music
starting a flash mob dance, inviting several
others to dance, two light up cigarettes and

joints to smoke and walk outside, while some share junk food and chat about their...

Amusing Accents

Note: Sample music is soft with dances, when the 2 following sonnets are spoken, but gets louder with wilder dancing towards the end of break. Group can move into the audience to get them to join the dance if possible.

Search YouTube for samples:

For background (soft) with dancing, during Amusing Accents below:

Music Sample: Fitness dance fun 'Turn up the music' http://youtu.be/dRWPjgLQ-0M

Student 2: Why would locals learn a foreign language?
Canadian English is enough. Twitching
My mouth, If listeners can somehow gauge
The background...
Student 1: I think training for switching
Education, class, country and culture
Is achievable with his skilled training...
Student 3: So voice can indicate background. Future
Opportunities are...
Student 2: Entertaining!

If Europeans sound Ameri<u>can</u>,
Africans like Canadian, and so f<u>orth</u>.
<u>Student 3:</u> Nut wise, a pistachio can be
pe<u>can</u>.
It should be useful and fun In ret<u>ort</u>,
<u>Student 1:</u> People judge intelligence by
ac<u>cent</u>.
In employment, it can help one's as<u>cent</u>.

*Left Side: Red Light district with red lamp
and bench, now looks like Hell with flames
and flashing lights, thunder sound effects*

<u>Storyteller:</u> In the meanwhile, The Trader
has encountered The Prostitute, who is now
dressed in a devilish outfit, at her territory
on the city streets, the hellishly wicked and
hot Red Light district, where they
experience a sexy vertical dance in a...

One Night Stand.

Note: The Trader takes off his shirt shows off his
torso with tattoos to The Prostitute. They dance like
a couple then exit after the sonnet or intermission
break.
For background of (soft) One Night Stand below:

Music Sample: Hell http://youtu.be/SD4ZoM2Qh10

It was lust at first sight both admitted
To each other and soon after chatting
Briefly, they met in life and committed
Instant one night stand sex. Without matting,
Their first act, a vertical position
With her pushed against an imagined wall,
He pumped her. This unusual decision
Was due to impatience. They did not fall
Though their legs wobbled. Strangers confusion
Of what to do after fornication
Made them forego social introduction.
Both wondered if future altercation
Can be thwarted by anonymity.
Both felt relief it was a big city.

Note: The Prostitute and The Trader in sexy dance.
Music Sample: Kizomba dance
http://youtu.be/SduFmaILPtY
or
Music Sample: Too Darn Hot ballet jazz
http://youtu.be/ftcvWY0La80

Storyteller: Meanwhile back in the class

room, The Students who came to life as dancers continue to release their pent up energy in a group dance, and The Trader and The Prostitute continue dancing entwined.

Music sample: LMFAO http://youtu.be/A762Ztl1ThY
Note: Play loud until the end of ten minutes of the Afternoon Break. After, Students sit down to relax.

<u>Storyteller:</u> During the same ten minutes break, Professor Wroth joins his colleagues at the Teachers Lounge. The other Teachers are discussing their goals and roles and rationalize about their positions in this new private foreign students school in

Note: Maybe dim the lights slightly in the class room below, and light up the lounge above.

[The Teachers]
Scene: Colleagues Collusion.

<u>Business Teacher:</u> As teachers, we vote that int<u>egration</u>
Be our common goal to achieve mainst<u>ream</u>

Levels of subjects. No segregation
Of foreign students to achieve this dream!
P.E. Teacher: Math, Science, P.E.,
Business and Language
Taught to foreigners who are ignorant
In English. Without exams who can gauge
Them or us?
Science Teacher: Local born or immigrant
Treated equally by our Faculty
Free to teach without accreditation
Degrees and diplomas.
Math Teacher: Difficulty
Caused by tests replaced by meditation
And peace of mind.
Business Teacher: Colleagues in collusion,
We'll participate without collision.

Science Teacher: Gibberish or Jargon?
Specific words, known to an insider,
Knowledgeable in explaining subjects
Are so puzzling to every outsider.
Math Teacher: Theories, names of
concepts and objects
In Math, Science, P.E., Business jargon
Need to be taught. Learning to memorize

And comprehend complexities --
Professor: Dragon
Slaying of ignorance, daunting by size,
Words unknown in foreign languages
Saint George accomplished such a miracle!
Business Teacher: The odds of winning, to bet one's wages
Adult foreigners can learn...
Math Teacher: Oracle
Predictions are meaning by semantics
Will be logical, not foolish antics.

Math Teacher: Numbers and Letters?
Attention to lessons leaves them...number?
Boredom and ignorance could both let her
Petrify instead of grow. A number
Is the same in the world, but a letter
Changes in each country. To calculate
By a mathematical formula
A solution is found. Will chocolate
Solve learning problems, gain matricula,
Give opportunities and employment?
Learning numbers leads to jobs in banking,
Engineering contracts, debt repayment,
Statistics estimations, accounting

Taxes. Her figure shape in Algebra?
Thirty six, twenty six, ___ like a zebra.

Storyteller: The Math Teacher seemed to
be insinuating without naming the female
student as he gestured an hourglass figure
shape while staring at Professor Wroth,
who was listening while eating a sandwich .

Science Teacher: Classification Conflict?
The Teachers Lounge, not cafeteria,
Is a place where having any degree
Allows one in. Avoiding bacteria
From food or students without pedigree
Is just like segregation by species!
Destiny by stars and Astronomy
Or by free will... They travelled over seas
Guided by stars and world economy,
Eager to learn out of curiosity.
Though separated, gradual osmosis
Permeates knowledge.
Professor: The atrocity
Obeyed like the Commandments from
Moses!
Science Teacher: Will we all harden in
petrifaction

The Professor's Lessons   Page 79

Or give in, soften by putrefaction?

Physical Education Teacher: Positive Energy!
Living thrives on positive energy,
Strength, endurance, nutrition, fitness, health.
Individual versus team synergy
Cooperate or compete in such stealth
Befitting survival of the fittest.
Diverse physiques: colour, muscle, weight, height,
They pass any standard physical test.
Mental, emotional, prepared to fight
Illness and weakness. Whether pass or fail,
P.E. has dance, games, sports, track and field,
Sociable tasks involve male and female.
To build confidence, a win or yield
In defeat, they learn that running the race
Matters, whether to save face or disgrace.

Business Teacher: Negative Negotiations?
Avoid negative negotiations
Among ourselves! Let us give credit

To teachers like ourselves. Whoever shuns
Foreign students are afraid they debit
By learning information, but commerce
For products and trading on a global
Level improve that all schools should
immerse
Students to make it easier. Trouble
In dealing, both in export and import,
Contracts, agreements, documentation,
Must be curbed and understood. To deport
Any immigrant? The lamentation
At the loss of their potential money
Conversions is worth keeping harmony!

Math Teacher: Social Intercourse?
Poverty and ignorance in Third World
Countries, overpopulation a curse,
These problems are solved by migrating.
Whirled
By such opportunities, intercourse
Socially and culturally opens
Possibilities that friendships, even
Marriages will bridge the gap.
Business Teacher: It deepens
Trade partnerships...

Professor: ...brings earth close to heaven,
Peace without wars.
Science Teacher: Diversity broadens
Minds, human understanding and wisdom,
While narrow racist prejudice deadens
Hearts.
Professor: Who can leave the foreign
students dumb
From ignorance and speechless, like
oysters
In closed shells or nuns sheltered in
cloisters?

Science Teacher: Peer Pride!
Celebrate education, prestigious
By mental and social accomplishment,
Mingling with peers in pride. How egregious
Not to have a degree...
Professor: ...a banishment
By Coventry, where Lady Godiva
Paraded nude to protest taxation,
Ignored by most, but Peeping Tom. Diva
That she was, despite townsfolk vexation,
She achieved her goal convincing husband.
Math Teacher: Education has status and
respect.

P.E. Teacher: It should be applauded like a brass band
Passing for all ears to hear.
Business Teacher: To expect
Rewards and awards, our duty to raise
Minds not lower, deserves Society's praise.

Professor: English Second Language!
England is ahead of China and Spain
Because of the Commonwealth, U.S.A.,
And Canada. All efforts and past pain
In expanding the network, an essay
Of adventure and imperialism
Could be written. People are now willing
To learn despite past colonialism!
Math Teacher: Knowledge to learn it is worth each shilling,
Pound and dollar.
Professor: It gives one confidence
By intelligence and vast connections
In the world.
Business Teacher: Investing brings dividends,
So schools, companies communications...
Professor: Use English as the main primary tool

The Professor's Lessons   Page 83

Developing one as a sage, not a fool.

Storyteller: Professor Wroth stood up and left his colleagues after his parting words, to return to the class. The Chairman of the ESL Board with his Assistant arrive for an

                    Intrusion Inquisition.
Assistant: Teachers, we disturb by intrusion
With The Chairman's entry into this Lounge.
Chairman: Noises from the class room caused confusion
To neighbours. Foreign students do not scrounge
For funding, paying by private sources
But it does not mean their misbehaviour
Is excusable! The school's resources,
Facility and staff need a saviour
Like me to control and manage daily.
Chaos results without supervision!
All of you will be questioned. To dally
With Teachers or Students, a revision
Of your contracts will exclude all social
Contact, by orders of this Field Marshall.

[The Chairman]
Scene: Chairman's Consternation

Storyteller: After the Afternoon Break,
The Students had already turned off the
boom box and were sitting down as
Professor Wroth returns from the Teachers
Lounge, unaware of what fun his class was
up to! The Chairman of the ESL Board is
heading towards the class room. He had
received neighbours complaints about the
noise coming from the ESL class room.
The Chairman and his Assistant had visited
the Teachers Lounge first to find out which
Teacher could be responsible. They reach
the door of the class room and knock at the
window of the door to be let in!

Credit FreeSFX Door Knocks
http://www.freesfx.co.uk/rx2/mp3s/7/7765_13473651
48.mp3

Chairman: Let me in! Open this door!

Storyteller: The Professor goes to the door
to open it. But the angry fat Chairman
cannot get through the door! He gets

stuck unfortunately at the doorway trying to force his way in. His small Assistant tries to push him through from his back.

Chairman: Professor Wroth! Please help me get in this doorway. I must talk to you and your class about the noise complaints I received from the neighbours.

Poetess (unseen voice): Professor Wroth, the noises are the students' voices and expressions of their primitive wild natures released by dancing to music.

Professor: Noises? I gave them a ten minute recess Break and they were seated quietly waiting when I returned. Let us try to pull you in. I will ask a student. Mario? Please assist the Board Chairman in and grab his hands and arms to pull him in.

Chairman: I am stuck in between inside and outside. Please do what you can to get me in or out.

Storyteller: The four struggled until The Professor decided to just go through the wall magically and suggest to The Assistant outside and The Chairman to try going in sideways instead of forcing him in, but finally she pushed him thru the doorway as he screamed in pain.

Credit FreeSFX Shout
http://www.freesfx.co.uk/rx2/mp3s/4/4687_13312998 23.mp3

Storyteller: Back inside the class room, The Professor introduces The Chairman.

Professor: Class please stand and greet him. This is Chairman Max, of the ESL Board of Directors.

ESL Students: Good afternoon Chairman Max!

Chairman: It is actually Chairman William Von Max. But thank you all for greeting me. I am visiting you today because of

Chairman: Complaints By Principle. Neighbours phone calls arrived by reception.

Loud music blasting from the foreign class
Room! Hard to believe that this deception
Is true seeing all so quiet, alas!
This is an adult English class. Foreign
Students from around the world pay tuition.
Lessons are taught whether in sun or rain.
The reputation of institution
Is based on administration and staff.
Our new licence to operate this school
Depends on strict standards. Please do not
laugh.
Take it seriously. I enforce the rule.
I was once a public school principal.
I followed standards, knew each principle.

Professor: Chairman, I can see they are all
so behaved in their seats. Surely there
must be some mistake!

Assistant: We received several angry
phone calls and recorded a few. The
Chairman wanted to come here right away
to check if any were true.

Storyteller: Chairman Von Max frowned
unsure, as he stared at the class of foreign

students. He fanned himself to cool his temper down as he stared bemused at his assistant and the students. He then decided to believe what his eyes could see, their polite behaviour, instead of the phone calls from the neighbours complaints.

Chairman: Okay. I apologize. It could be a misunderstanding. There is a new foreign exhibition of ancient civilization. Please, as part of my sincere apology, take them on a field trip outside to the

Chairman: Museum And Artifacts.
If you could show them the excavation
For recovered artifacts by slide show.
Displays of museums preservation
Of civilizations from wars of woe
Include: huge fossils of brontosaurus,
Statues of ancient Mesopotamia,
Babylon and Assyria. Thesaurus,
Dictionary, online Wikipedia
Are tools for research and definition.
Ask, if a culture is taken away
From its people, will balanced opinion
Or biased decide? Researchers who sway

The public about cultures Arabic,
Sometimes depict Arabs as barbaric!

Storyteller: The class of Students stood up,
clapped and cheered, excited for the field
trip together to the museum.

Chairman: Good! I am glad we have
resolved our misunderstanding. Now I
have to go. Please assist me thru the door.

Storyteller: The Professor decided to make
it easy for all and motioned towards the wall
near the door since he had the power to go
thru walls and allow others too if he wanted.

Professor: Yes, follow me. This way is
easier for you.

Storyteller: The Professor went thru the
front wall and gestured for The Chairman to
follow and both of them were soon outside.
The small Assistant went out the door. They

said their good byes. The Chairman and
Assistant went along the sidewalk outside
and The Professor returned to the class
room.

[The Lovers]

*Mini Set Right: the male's living room with
a laptop using Skype web cam, he is on
stage and female is on web cam projection
screen behind*
*Back Screen: changes image depending
on reality or fantasy*

Professor: Well I hope you enjoyed your
break and can now pay attention to
dialogues between the fourth Characters,
The Lovers. I will show their progression
through different stages from: meeting,
courtship, proposal, marriage, adultery,
separation, to reunification. The other
Characters have monologues recalling their
personal and professional experiences,
whereas The Lovers, are a couple full of
imagination in their heads and hearts acting
out dialogues of their...

Professor: Fantasies, Lies.
With imagination, a pretty <u>maid</u>
Becomes beautiful. With mesmer<u>ism</u>
She even becomes an ocean mer<u>maid</u>
With scales and fins. In anti-rac<u>ism</u>
Foreigners pretend to be more flipp<u>ant</u>
Than they are. In love, attractive <u>moochers</u>
Make holes in lovers pockets, though
mord<u>ant</u>
They might be. In fun, many lip s<u>moochers</u>
Steal moist kisses, without a forfei<u>ture</u>
Of their partners. In divorce, a forl<u>orn</u>
Mate may sue for alimony fu<u>ture</u>.
Although she might be caught in-between
t<u>orn</u>
In half by unreal, foolish fantas<u>ies</u>
Of better partners or living more l<u>ies</u>.

Professor: Using the modern tools of
communication on the internet via Skype
web cam, The Lovers finally decide to have
a real life

Future Meeting.
Female: After months of chatting on a
vir<u>tual</u>

Level, let's make plans towards our m<u>eeting</u>
In reality, hoping our mu<u>tual</u>
Attraction will continue.
<u>Male:</u> My gr<u>eeting</u>
Will welcome you warmly! Like old l<u>overs</u>
In a novel. Let's laugh looking for<u>ward</u>
to our future meeting.
<u>Female:</u> No stop <u>overs</u>.
Soon as I land, I am heading to<u>ward</u>
Your place.
<u>Male:</u> I worry, Maybe a pub<u>lic</u>
Place would be best. I am only r<u>enting</u>
In an old building.
<u>Female:</u> I hope we will c<u>lick</u>
In reality. Whatever inv<u>enting</u>
We did will then be revealed! Any l<u>ies</u>
We concealed we will for sure rea<u>lize</u>.

Left Side: with lamp and bench
Back Screen : airport or train station?

Note: She walks in, he walks over to meet her and
he carries her suitcase.

<u>Professor:</u> She travels to meet him,
because from his kind generosity and male

curiosity, he extends to her his

Kind Invitation.

Male: On arrival, my kind invitation
As a stranger, without your denial,
If my humble tower's elevation
May uplift you, or if I on trial
Accused for such suggestion shall suffer
Punishment, then let silence embarrass
None.

Female: Smiling I ask, will there be
supper?
For my acceptance forgives to harass
You from hunger. It was unbearable
The distance and time to meet in person!
Do steer me past the crowd's noisy rabble.

Male: Let me drive a damsel to my prison.
Feed her food. Although we are fastidious,
The pleasure outweighs tasks which are
tedious!

Right Mini Set: his apartment living room
Note: They enter, sit on his couch facing each other.

Professor: She stays as his guest and as
they become acquainted in courtship and

more serious, they have a heart to heart talk in his apartment. For him, enjoying his bachelor state, a relationship involves risk in a

Love Gamble.

Male: Gambling for money or love may surfeit
Risks. Butterflies inside make one queasy
Enough opportunity is forfeit.
Monopoly, Roulette, and Parcheesi
Involve luck and skill. A poor pariah
Is a lonely loser who importunes
Anyone for help. To be a pasha
Lover, one courts and hunts many fortunes
Until one succeeds. The luck of the dice
Is like God's blessing causing delirious
Joy upon winning! Those who do entice,
Await the right moment to taste luscious
Luxury or love. Money's parity
To love may also have disparity.

Professor: For her, love grows like a garden filling their souls

Bare Necessities.

<u>Female:</u> In personal relationships, mistr<u>ust</u>
Of a partner is a frightening th<u>ought</u>.
Intimacy and love require one m<u>ust</u>
Be worthy of secrets, cannot be b<u>ought</u>
With money to betray a lover's f<u>aith</u>,
Be responsible, good, honest, m<u>ature</u>,
And loving enough to carry one's w<u>eight</u>.
Like a plant, a relationship's n<u>ature</u>
Needs care and attention. To blossom,
s<u>eeds</u>
Have to be nurtured with a loving tou<u>ch</u>
To sprout into full grown plants. Pull out
w<u>eeds</u>
That stifle growth. Like any flower pat<u>ch</u>,
Full of life, colours and scents, our souls
b<u>are</u>
Necessities when met, last wear and t<u>ear</u>.

<u>Storyteller:</u> Reaching mutual understanding
of each other's expectations, they hug and
kiss like lovers.

<u>Professor:</u> Let us freeze The Lovers for a
moment so you can all come closer to view
them. I will allow you to go through the
walls of our class room to get a closer look

at The Lovers. Here they are locked in a kiss and embrace, giving into their physical and sexual instincts after reaching a mental agreement. Although for humans love can happen all year round and there usually is

No Mating Season.

Note: Frozen Moment 1 as The Professor talks below, his class stand and move closer to the living room surrounding The Lovers who are frozen in an embrace and kiss sitting on the couch. Lightning and thunder sounds as The Students go through the wall.
Credit FreeSFX Thunder rumble 22s
http://www.freesfx.co.uk/rx2/mp3s/1/943_1245800784.mp3

Poetess (unseen voice): The four seasons of Spring, Summer, Autumn and Winter depending on a country's climate and weather are stimulating to the five senses for mating: smell, sight, sound, taste and touch. Even the sixth sense can be a hidden radar to detect sexual love signals.

Professor: Single-hood is a lifestyle for loners

Who by fate or choice decided that life
Is meant for self development. Lovers
And couples, pairing as husband and wife
Are thus either envied or avoided.
Loneliness and hot dreams that are sexual
Can disturb a sad spinster to blush red,
As with shy bachelors. Without sensual
Stimulation from the opposite sex,
The hormones for attracting a partner
Are lost. Animal lust will no more vex
Nor drive the person into a corner,
Trapped by nature during mating season
To seek any partner beyond reason.

Professor: Class, you can return to your
seats and face their living room set to
continue watching.

Mini Set: same living room set for the rest

Professor: Now they are considering their
relationship and future. Their marriage
Proposal has two scenarios: first showing
where he was forced into proposing
marriage instead of living common law in
reality by

Choice Or Convenience?

Female: Darling, is it not time you should propose?

Male: Propose what?

Storyteller: He gulped a sweet chocolate.

Female: Marriage of course!

Storyteller: Intrigued, he struck a pose.

Male: What? For a bachelor, it is too late!

Storyteller: She stared.

Female: Really? Surely we have options,
The future...

Male: Together? What ever for?

Female: A marriage for practical solutions:
To own property, raise children before...

Male: You get pregnant? If we have a marriage,
I literally will lose...

Female: Your freedom?
If we move in together, the outrage
Of family, neighbours...

Male: That is a dumb
Idea! We should tie the knot by choice.
Invite them to our wedding to rejoice!

Back Screen: farm plantation estate

Music: Black Magic Woman instrumental
http://youtu.be/1Tle02SQ1cs start at 0:10 after the
first line of the Male

<u>Professor:</u> This second Proposal in his
head, is set in a farm plantation where he
pretends to be a rich Hispanic Don in a
fantasy of

       Don Juan's Banana.
<u>Male:</u> Among men, I must be your number
<u>one</u>!

Music Sample: http://youtu.be/1Tle02SQ1cs start
at 0:10 and time words below with music ending at
2:49

<u>Storyteller:</u> (0:34) He peels and offers her a
ban<u>ana</u>
From his Brazilian plantation, Don J<u>uan</u>
A rich landlord. Music of Sant<u>ana</u>
Played.
<u>Male:</u> (1:00) I export fruits: mango,
pine<u>apple</u>,
Banana. Maybe you seek happ<u>iness</u>
In life?
<u>Female:</u> (1:24) Do you import orange,

<u>apple</u>?
I like those fruits too, tasting their
sweet<u>ness</u>.
<u>Storyteller:</u> (1:46) Watching her eat his
banana, he sm<u>iled</u>.
She smiles back looking deep into his <u>eyes</u>.
<u>Male:</u> (2:10) We will marry soon. I have
never <u>lied</u>
To you, so be faithful. 'I will hire sp<u>ies</u>
To be sure...'
<u>Female:</u> (2:32) As your wife, all our <u>feelings</u>
Will be uncovered as these fruit p<u>eelings</u>!

*Back Screen: estate mansion with a
carriage or a python?*

<u>Professor:</u> In their marriage, as a husband,
he has fantasies of being a rich man with a
beautiful wife. He shows his jealousy of her
possible infidelity by purchasing a

Python In The Phaeton.
<u>Male:</u> I expect obedience as instru<u>ctor</u>
Of my loving wife.
<u>Storyteller:</u> Born to a we<u>althy</u>
Family, he purchased a constri<u>ctor</u>,

A python to strangle her if fealty
Is not observed by her. Under the seat
Of the phaeton, he keeps it.
Male: Our marriage
Is satisfactory, I hope?
Storyteller: The heat
Inside stirs the serpent in the carriage.
Female: Of course, my Mister. I am quite
content
With the house, our lifestyle, our sacred
vows.
You rescued me from struggles, discontent,
And I am grateful.
Male: Do you think that cows
Go mad when their bulls wander far away,
With mouths frothing, getting sores, while at
play?

Back Screen: haystack in a barn or office

Professor: He uses control as he pretends
to be a rich CEO of a corporation,
searching for any sign of her infidelity like a

Hairpin In A Haystack.
Male: As your spouse I observed that

beautiful
Wives married rich men and I classified
Myself in that category – rich fool
In love with beauty. Though your class defied
Mine, I married you darling – a show piece
Of a woman. I imposed rules, curfews,
And schedules on our joint lives to appease
My jealous streak. As my wife, don't confuse
My organization with your background.
My status is yours and they will respect
You as the Boss wife.
Storyteller: Many years, he found
Satisfaction with their marriage – no speck
Of scandal, nor hairpin in a hay stack
Gave him cause for a possessive attack.

Back Screen of Left: Red Light District

Note: The Male is with The Prostitute sitting on the park bench under the red lamp.

Professor: Although she is a faithful wife, he sometimes goes out alone to the Red Light District for a

A Few Drinks.

Prostitute: Drink more alcohol. With a few more drinks
I will look okay to you too. I poured
You a shot of whiskey.

Male: My love life stinks.
My wife and children are tired of me, bored
By our routines.

Prostitute: I understand your woes.
Men and women come to drink and forget.

Male: I work and support them. I have no foes.
But strangers still see me as a target
To push around. So, I try to avoid
Them.

Prostitute: I touch your arm, warm in sympathy.
If you need my comfort when paranoid,
Visit me. Your family's apathy
Is appalling! Please drink while snickering.

Male: I will, as it beats my wife's bickering!

Note: The Female, his wife had followed and sees him with The Prostitute drinking outside on the street

Storyteller: Unknown to him, his wife had

followed him and saw him sharing drinks with The Prostitute in the Red Light District.

Professor: Class, come closer again to see the husband being unfaithful with The Prostitute who has offered him alcohol drinks outside on a street bench, where unknown to him his wife watches from the shadows where he has a

Note: Frozen Moment 2 with the male drinking alcohol with The Prostitute outside on a bench under the lamp with The Prostitute sitting on his lap and his wife is standing watching from the shadows.

Girl On Lap.

Professor: Jealousy rears its fangs at misfortune
Of catching in the act an unfaithful
Lover. Infidelity's opportune
Moments are taken by horns, but a fool
Is apprehended. Why seek the public's
Attention, approval? Adultery
Is for the discreet, state most republics
And nations. A love expert's mastery
Involves secrecy and intimacy.
A lover's lap is just as hot alone

As in a crowd. Sexual delic<u>acy</u>
Involves public decorum. A sigh, m<u>oan</u>
From a kiss, and embrace, leaves us
re<u>signed</u>
To hiding pleasures, as the under<u>signed</u>.

Note: The Male leaves The Prostitute. The Female
returns to their apartment where she gets drunk on
the couch; The Professor and The Students return to
their class to watch both sides -- on one the wife
getting drunk, on the other The Gossip laughing
with The Prostitute.

<u>Storyteller:</u> The Gossip, a friend of The
Prostitute had noticed this scenario, and
related her view of the story to her friend
after, describing her as

Chicken Gibbet.

<u>Gossip:</u> Fouler than foul, entrails, gut and
gibl<u>et</u>
Carved out of the poor, frail, love-sick
chic<u>ken</u>,
Who pining for her love, on a gibb<u>et</u>
Did hang, her foolish heart and neck
bro<u>ken</u>.
Spying one night, she witnessed imbrogli<u>o</u>,

Angered by jealousy, her mate's gimm<u>ick</u>
To test fidelity, trust. Gigol<u>o</u>
That he was, he drove this poor love-bird
s<u>ick</u>,
Drinking with some chick near a honky-t<u>onk</u>
Bar. Sadly, this flirtatious d<u>alliance</u>
Upset her; she drank alcohol till <u>zonked</u>.
<u>Prostitute:</u> Motto: 'When bound happy in
<u>alliance</u>,
Do not mistrust, nor test love, nor d<u>ally</u>,
As some curious cat in a drunk's <u>alley</u>.'

<u>Storyteller:</u> The Prostitute and The Gossip
laugh at The Lovers and their troubled
relationship.

Credit FreeSFX   Female Laugh
http://www.freesfx.co.uk/rx2/mp3s/4/4717_13313026
14.mp3

Mini Set Right: Living room
Note: The Female alone with gift wrap and presents
sings missing her husband, The Male.

<u>Professor:</u> After that drinking incident, The
Lovers separated in the summer until the
winter, she remains living in the apartment

but does not know where he has gone after their argument. So in December, she misses him because

Christmas Is Here.
<u>Female:</u> Christmas is here,
And I'm lonely for you
There's a fire burning bright
In the fireplace tonight...
Snow on the ground
Will never fall so purely, again!
I'm thinking of you, my love
So far away...
All the gifts are wrapped
Love it means forever!
Will you call me sometime
Before December's over?
Merry Christmas, darling!
Hope you'll come home
Really soon
And melt the ice
That entered our lives
Last June
Till then my love
I'll be wrapping presents in my arms...

Back Screen: him alone in his family estate

Professor: Class, please come closer to
their living room where The Lovers are
separated physically. The wife is left behind
depressed, and the husband is far away on
his family's estate overseas. However,
although they are separated physically,
being The Lovers, there remains between
them a mental, emotional and spiritual

Note: Frozen Moment 3 the female is in their living
room sulking and thinking of him, he is far away in
an estate also unhappy thinking and missing her.

Professor: Love Energy.
Emotions between them flowed constantly
Entering their insides in reactions
Like two batteries feeding instantly,
Empowering their thoughts, words, and
actions.
If he felt romantic and wonderful,
She would adjust to his mood uplifted
By his passionate presence. Powerful
Feelings immersed them as lovers lifted
With empathy able to feel the same
Simultaneously. Even when apart

Telepathy connected them. Their <u>aim</u>
Was to remain lovers each life, take <u>part</u>
In soul reincarnations for<u>ever</u>.
Reuniting lovers never s<u>ever</u>.

Mini Set: the living room with a laptop
Back Screen: a Skype web cam session

Note: She walks out and returns pregnant (pillow) to
the apartment, to start a Skype web cam session
with him at his family estate.

<u>Professor:</u> Realizing she is pregnant, she
calls him over Skype and informs him of the
news, giving him an ultimatum to choose
or she will divorce him in

Your Last Day.
<u>Female:</u> If you don't come, consider this
your <u>last</u> Day!
<u>Storyteller:</u> His wife's threatening ultima<u>tum</u>
With a glare and pointed finger, a<u>las</u>
Made him pause.
<u>Male:</u> But those at work do pres<u>ume</u>
I will attend. I have oblig<u>ations</u>.
A picnic social with your club is n<u>ext</u>

In importance. 'Our deal negotiations
Ride on Sunday meetings.' I'm quoting text
Of my boss.
Female: I mean it. You either pick
Me -- your wife and partner, or co-workers!
Male: Let me think...weighing priorities,
'Sick!
Sorry, can't go.'
Storyteller: He lifted his wife's curse
By sending this text to work. He saved their
Marriage, including their upcoming heir!

Note: He returns to their living room, they embrace.

Professor: The Lovers reunite after this
because of the pregnancy and their future
baby. He returns to his wife, finally realizing

　　　Life's Important Experiences.
Male: Birth, baptism, communion,
graduation
Employment, marriage, pregnancy are life's
Meaningful experiences. Creation
Is celebrated by events. A wife's
Companionship can make memorable
Moments. Family, friends, acquaintances

And strangers are all inescapable,
Bonded by love and blood. No distances
Can separate us from our destiny
And our relationships. Humanity
Progresses with meaning. A mutiny
From all others deprives community
Of an individual. We should live full
Lives because if not, one becomes a fool.

Professor: Together again, the husband
weighs the shame of being a rich fool
tricked into marriage, versus remaining a
bachelor fool who misses out on life's
experiences, deciding marriage is better
than single-hood for him with a wife, who is
also jealous yet faithful like him.

Note: The Lovers exit with the mini set; the next
mini set is for The Leaders.

[The Leaders]
[The Queen with The General]

Mini Set Right: 4 tea tables with 4 chairs
Back Screen: Royal Palace and Grounds,
horses in background

Professor: Now for the fifth Characters,
The Leaders, a powerful role played by
Royals, Presidents, and Generals who are
responsible for the vision of a nation and its
people, seeing the

View From The Top.

Storyteller: As Professor Wroth speaks, he
illustrates the pyramid points and connects
the dots with lines to form it on white board.

Professor: Words used as a source of
inspiration
To propel the people as a nation,
Giving value to their perspiration
To succeed despite their desperation...
The pyramid point centralized power
Expected on the great appointed hour.
Every leader had to climb the tower
To be obeyed below the base of four
Points, where the public listened to the
speech.
All raised their humble heads to hear him
teach
Wisdom from the peak. But failing, impeach

The cruel proud braggart beyond their reach.
He must have vision to reach the zenith
Or his bones crushed at the nadir's granite!

<u>Professor:</u> The Pyramid is a typical power structure showing how one person at the top rules over the bottom people. This is true for political, business and financial organizations. As a Leader, The Queen, a Royal who is raised to inherit the role of power, has an extensive social circle including other Royals, wealthy people, and other Leaders as special guests. She discusses politics at her tea parties allowing her guests the privilege of the insiders view with

The Queen's Glimpse.

Music: Her Majesty's Music
http://www.allmusic.com/performance/trumpet-tune-mq0000610548
Note: Minor characters, including The Lovers as guests, bring flowers and gifts to present to The Queen, and The Maid is also present nearby with other royal servants serving tea and pastries.

<u>Storyteller:</u> While the royal music is playing in the background, the special guests are presented to The Queen giving their gifts and bowing and curtsying to her, then sitting at the tables. The Professor is also a special guest sitting with The Lovers and The Chairman. At The Queen's center table, The Queen sits only with The General.

<u>Queen:</u> Meandering along my palace grounds,
As Queen, I survey my greenhouse and farm.
Where are my royal horses and pet hounds?
I would like to show them to guests. With charm,
I entertain them at dinner parties,
Concerned about their health and present state.
Later, I read letters, and over teas
With Generals at my royal estate,
We discuss politics. How to appeal
To local farmers and new immigrants?
Perhaps, racist quota limits repeal,

And increase foreigners and farmers
grants?
Announce to every Commonwealth nation
To celebrate Diamond Coronation!

Storyteller: As a special guest in this royal
tea party, The Professor has an insider's
view of the mixing of social, economic
and political topics that The Queen, and
other Leaders such as The General,
discuss and make policies to improve
situations of the people while having

Royal Tea
General: In honour, build a royal
monument
Of devotion to The Queen, observant,
Erudite with charming temperament.
She impresses me much, this humble
servant,
With her noble, powerful dignity.
Queen: My ceremonies, comedy-drama,
Serious and gay in world community:
Hear the historical diorama--
Invite a male political despot
For a wonderful lunch, perhaps a bite

Of delicious cake; with English tea pot
Brew a peaceful revolution, incite
Constitution over a cup of tea.
To refuse, one commits lese majesty.

Storyteller: In the Commonwealth, tea and
other trade has bonded participating
nations and peoples in a global trade
network. Those who remain in good terms
with the political and economical trade are
immigrants and locals and considered as

Loyal Subjects.
General: The Commonwealth network
does empower
Its member nations with the leadership
Of The Queen with vision from a tower.
Queen: Individuals with good citizenship
Enter Public Service under command
Of Government. Responsibility
Towards country and God meet the demand
Depending on one's capability.
Foreigners achieve nationality
Following laws as obedient subjects.
For a sociable personality
Our multiculturalism rejects

Racists believing human loyalty
And equality.
General: We serve royalty.

Storyteller: As part of the Commonwealth,
member nations can apply for immigration
and citizenship in Canada, a designated
country for multiculturalism. Here the
seriousness of respecting the process of
genuine application resulted in an

Immigration Bill C-31.
General: In June, approved by the House
of Commons,
This new Bill entered the House of Senate
To be debated, then Royal summons
Queen: Will decide the ultimate legal fate
Of the lowest class of poor immigrants.
False claims mean that officers could
deport
Foreigners or imprison. Welfare grants,
Medical treatments cut off, the airport
Is safer than jail for war refugees!
Cruel governments sometimes persecute
Ethnic minorities, ending their lease
On the land or if needed,

<u>General:</u> ex<u>ecute</u>
Them and instead of protect, impri<u>son</u>
Along with smugglers, who commit trea<u>son</u>!

<u>Storyteller:</u>   Royalty has its history and The
Queen decides to relate a historical incident
involving another Royal, The King of the
Vandals tribe. Refer to Wikipedia on the
455 Sack of Rome for further reading.
Refer to:
http://en.wikipedia.org/wiki/Sack_of_Rome_(455)
This was motivated by avengeance on
behalf of another Royal, a King of the Holy
Roman Empire as requested by his widow
Queen in the

Diatribe Of A Tribe.

Note: The Queen reads from paper to The General.

<u>Queen:</u> Rumours of the King's death did
flabber<u>gast</u>
His ally, King Genseric. Sc<u>andalized</u>,
"Our marriage treaty is voided!" A<u>ghast</u>,
He marched to Rome to loot not v<u>andalize</u>.
"We will take gold and silver to a<u>venge</u>
Valentinian. Huneric will m<u>arry</u>

Eudocia as planned. And for re<u>venge</u>,
Maximus death by mob! We shall c<u>arry</u>
Our treasures without harming inhabi<u>tants</u>,
As Pope Leo implored." So, the V<u>andals</u>
Obeyed to sack Rome, following his <u>taunts</u>.
"Add this to the Holy Roman sc<u>andals</u>.
Breaking a betrothal", his dia<u>tribe</u>,
"Is akin to betrayal of our <u>tribe</u>!"

<u>Storyteller:</u> Recalling how in the past,
Royal Kings led and fought their own
battles along with their warriors, and how in
the present, there are now Generals
appointed to protect a country from
invaders or fight wars overseas, The Queen
acknowledged the importance of her guest,

An American General.
<u>Queen:</u> Love for world peace led you to
h<u>eroic</u>
Afghanistan and Korean <u>missions</u>.
<u>General:</u> The goal of democracy met<u>eoric</u>
In lands where political re<u>missions</u>
Are due to disease of dictator<u>ships</u>!
<u>Queen:</u> Major General Champagne's
dev<u>otion</u>

Can lead troops, tanks, air planes and
battleships.
General: Faith and loyalty blend in emotion
Within men and women, even foreign.
God protects those who believe in
goodness,
Working in any weather, sun and rain.
Queen: Medals and awards should honour
and bless
You who passed every military test.
General: Falsehood ends with winners who
are honest!

Storyteller: The General lamented about
his job and the price of wars with soldiers
deaths overseas, both sides fighting for
their own reasons, shedding their own
blood, red as tulips and poppies in

Blood Red Fields.
General: Battlefields have stained blood
red the tulips
From vainglorious deaths of men. The
poppies
Have killed the mortal pain screamed from
red lips,

What price our lives in search of war not
peace!
Foreign and Afghan rebels and soldiers
Have fallen on the same fields sovereign,
Fighting decades with their aching
shoulders.
Streaming from lost faces are tears or rain.
Civilians fight their own military
As rebels terrorizing in bloody
Vengeance. Neither side feels solitary
In such loss and frustration. Nobody
Is safe on this territory of fields
Blossoming flowers with drops of blood
yields...

Storyteller: Stationed in overseas bases,
soldiers being like all red blooded men who
sometimes need women, The General
allowed them to leave the gates for visiting
women waiting outside. He sometimes
puzzled about such temporary relations
when opening such a

Gateway For Infidels.
Queen: The army is led by an obstinate
General who controls the labyrinth.

General: For security, I do desig<u>nate</u>
A gatekeeper to question in succ<u>inct</u>
Tone those who enter and leave.
Desp<u>erate</u>
Women enamoured in hum<u>iliation</u>,
Beg entry to mate, but I would b<u>erate</u>
Them. Why persist in such aff<u>iliation</u>
With brutes who shall bring you only
dis<u>grace</u>?
Are there no other men who subju<u>gate</u>
Women without falling from God's <u>grace</u>?
Women swoon waiting outside the locked
<u>gate</u>.
They long to bewitch men to leave and
<u>tempt</u>
Them to mate, despite their leader's
con<u>tempt</u>.

Storyteller: The Queen was amused by his
puzzlement and wondered whether he
himself had found anyone to unlock the

Key To His Heart.
Queen: Love is locked up in your heroic
<u>heart</u>.
All the battles you solved with enemies

Glad for peace.
General: Medals and awards brought hearth
And home, honour! My only nemesis
Is unhappy loneliness. Thus, in search
Of a partner, I travelled all countries,
Met many women as part of research.
Brave, I hiked through the forest for the trees.
If only I find a woman lonely,
Independent in her environment.
Will she unlock my heart? Be mine only?
Queen: Yes, if a real wedding ring ornament
Wraps her finger. A hero so daring
Seeks a forlorn wife, faithful and caring.

Storyteller: Embarrassed, The General tried to divert The Queen's attention towards a popular global issue being debated -- global warming. With the changing weather and its effect on animals and people, especially the growing heat temperatures, he noted that

The Ice Age Is Over.

General: The white bear knows that its day
is ending.
Ice islands are breaking with alarming
Increase due to global warming sending
Sun rays back to earth.

Queen: Even a charming
Politician noticed its life's distress
And filmed the "Inconvenient Truth" to save
The earth.

General: To clean the world from all its
mess
Is now a goal to end the harsh heat wave
Melting giant glaciers of the Ice Age.
All the planets in the Solar System
Keep on revolving despite this outrage,
With global cataclysms in rhythm.
After the snow melts, those who will survive
Will take care of the earth to stay alive.

Storyteller: The pessimism of The General
at a royal tea party darkened the
atmosphere, but as usual, The Queen gives
a hopeful message to The General and The
Public in

Let The Sun Shine.

Queen: Although there is valid cause for alarm

About the effects of global warming,

I as The Queen caution staff that more harm

Would arise if panic set in.

General: Charming

As usual, please speak.

Queen: Recall the rainbow

Shining after the Great Flood. Let the sun

Shine bright on Earth for flower seeds to grow.

Let the children play in the yards for fun.

God created the Heaven and the Earth.

Love and respect all creatures. Together

We will survive cataclysms, from birth

To death; we will adjust any weather

To suit our needs. Rain, snow, quake, storm and flood

Shall follow forecasts without shedding blood.

Storyteller: After the tea party, The Queen has other obligations towards her military so she stands up with The General and prepares with the assistance of one of her Maids in

Music: Her Majesty's Music
http://www.allmusic.com/performance/be-strong-of-good-courage-confortare-mq0000610553
Note: The Queen and The Maid are acting only.

[The Maid]

Note: The Maid brings out a large hand mirror for The Queen to look at herself, also assists with the Royal Red Garter or The General does it.

Storyteller: Maid And Her Queen.
The Queen admires herself, with fou du roi
Jewellery round her neck. Cupidity
Was a facet of her, which did annoy
Maid, whom Queen accused of stupidity.
Maid switched Queen's ornaments, as contagion,
With fake ones, pretending to be docile,
As she aided Queen. Queen's faithful legion
Were wanting honours for old wars, senile
As they were. Queen sent Maid to the garret
To fetch and place the Royal Red Garter,

On her thick thigh. It was coloured scar<u>let</u>
As blood shed in wars. Queen, of the b<u>arter</u>
Unaware, went on her way for geld<u>ing</u>
Military horses, warriors knight<u>ing</u>...

Note: The Queen and The General leave the set
followed by The Maid, ditto all The Guests depart.

[The Lawyer]

Mini Set: a law office with table, chairs
Back Screen of Mini Set: Law Office

Note: Sitting and waiting for consultation in his office
are: Tourist, Prostitute, Trader, and Gossip.

<u>Professor:</u> At last the sixth Character, The
Lawyer, who works in law offices and
Courts to advise people who are accused of
crimes both civil and criminal. Waiting for
consultation in his office are: The Tourist,
The Prostitute, The Trader, and The
Gossip. Dressed in formal black, lawyers,
police and even Judges are like ravens or

<u>Professor:</u>   Crows In Counsel.
Criminal court, men wearing gowns in

black,
Dressed up as steel-eyed ravens, donning wigs
Perch on high, judging each evil attack
On Good Society. Evidence as twigs,
Gathered till enough make prosecution
Probable, or else, costly civil suits
Have to be filed. Common prostitution,
Murder, rape, assault, burglary are roots
Of evil, which darken lives, black as crows.
Penalties are meted out by a Judge.
Compensation to victims on escrows
Until the verdict's read. If a big smudge
Taints good people's reputations, Counsel
Might advise the press not to kiss and tell.

Professor: In his law office, The Lawyer
has his clients sitting, waiting for their cases
to be reviewed and to listen to his advice.
In this case, The Lawyer reads that charges
were dropped, against The Tourist by a
Local who turned out to be The Prostitute,
from the understanding and kind

Note: Lawyer is sitting at his desk, reading from
case file folder to both who are sitting in front.

Whims Of A Judge.

Lawyer: You a foreigner accused of sexual
Assault by police who charged, arrested,
And imprisoned you without a trial.
The Judge reviewed the case,"Was he
tested
For his semen sample? A prostitute
Complains and why is he blamed for buying
Her? Maybe she is merely destitute,
Desperate to make some money. Trying
Him in Court would not be worthwhile. Just
drop
The charges." The Judge's finger had
landed
In 'no' not 'yes', using a fun game prop
Of 'eenie meenie miny mo'. Stranded
For an answer in small petty cases,
He used games, whims, and the Parties
faces.

Note: The Prostitute and The Tourist return to waiting
chairs, and the next case, The Trader sits at The
Lawyer's desk, and so on with The Gossip, taking
turns for his advice, then returning to waiting chairs.

Professor: The Trader has overheard
someone bragging on the island he retired

The Professor's Lessons   Page 130

in, about embezzling investors and
stockholders. The Lawyer repeats and
takes notes of his character witness story of

Chief Thief.

Trader: On the island, the Chief chosen by
vote
Was the wealthiest, most skilled in stealing.
Lawyer: He was crowned Chief of the
Thieves on this remote
Island. His ability in dealing
Dirty and robbing rich and poor alike,
Escaping police investigations,
Has increased his status. Taking a hike
Around, he was notorious in nations."
Trader: His rapt audience clapped,
congratulating
Him with cheers and jeers. "May you steal
without
Getting caught! Thrill us with titillating
Escapades of robberies as a lout
With loot."
Lawyer: He told them fun stories as thief,
How his experiences made him their Chief.
Professor: If an investigation is done on
The Chief based on The Trader's testimony,

it would need help from police operating
on the island based on the limitation of
jurisdiction, or international police Interpol.

Note: The Gossip sits in front of The Lawyer's desk.

Professor: The Gossip decides to confess
her motives to The Lawyer taking notes,
after being threatened by The Prostitute for
slandering her with a verbal

Stab In The Back.
Lawyer: When socializing, drop a
compliment
To gain the trust of people when
Gossip: envious
Of them.
Lawyer: Sympathize with sweet sentiment
If needed when
Gossip: sick.
Lawyer: When feeling devious,
Gossip: Spread a rumour about their
weaknesses:
Lawyer: Disease, failure, any confidential
Private information where witnesses
Are family and friends, providential

By confidence and intimacy, <u>trust</u>
To know secrets. One can hold a keen
kn<u>ife</u>
And spread butter on bread from face to
cr<u>ust</u>
<u>Gossip:</u> Or thrust it from the back. Death or
l<u>ife</u>
Is a battle of supremacy, t<u>ough</u>;
<u>Lawyer:</u> Both libel or slander are not
en<u>ough</u>?

<u>Professor:</u> To end the consultation session
with everyone, The Lawyer then asks them
to stand and he shares some wisdom on
civil and criminal crimes which occur in life
and if caught and found guilty before a trial,
the choice becomes

Jail Or Bail.
<u>Lawyer:</u> Life's experiences and
relation<u>ships</u>
Based on choices and personal<u>ity</u>
Sometimes lead to crimes. Both peace and
war <u>ships</u>
To defend or offend town and c<u>ity</u>
And all their peoples and terri<u>tories</u>

Are written in laws and enforced <u>order</u>
By Governments and Courts. The vic<u>tories</u>
In wars often cost lives on each b<u>order</u>.
For every winner, there is a los<u>er</u>.
For each criminal, there is a vic<u>tim</u>.
The prisons are full, ditto each shel<u>ter</u>.
For some live in light while others live d<u>im</u>.
Freedom is for all those who abhor <u>jail</u>
And follow laws, or who can afford b<u>ail</u>.

<u>Professor:</u> He then comforts them with the
possibility that former crimes can be
legalized through changes in public attitude
and Government legislation, using the
example of

Bill C-38 Civil Marriage Act.
<u>Lawyer:</u> Up to fourteen years of
imprison<u>ment</u>
In Criminal Law, now replaced with p<u>ride</u>,
A Bill legalizing what caused tor<u>ment</u>
For same gender relationships -- de<u>ride</u>
It no more those in heterosex<u>ual</u>
Church wedded bondings. A civil mar<u>riage</u>
Has replaced same sex affairs, past cas<u>ual</u>
And hidden liaisons. Gone the out<u>rage</u>

With pink triangle and rainbow parades!
Society now approves integration,
No longer needing secrets and charades.
Freedom to love from discrimination --
All members gain respect, equality,
Tolerance of homosexuality.

Note: All are embarrassed silent then exit his office.

PART THREE
Conclusion

Back in the central classroom

Storyteller: Returning to the class room
after watching the fictional Characters,
Professor Wroth concluded the lessons with
some wisdom from life's experiences.

Professor: Class, all The Characters have
presented scenarios or experiences of their
professional occupations. If you analyze
them from a moral point of view of right
from wrong, good from evil, some
experience the

Consequence Of Conscience.

Professor: Morality, ethics, and right from wrong
Can influence actions of intentions.
Human nature can be quite weak or strong
Depending on our traits and pretensions.
With such a conscience, we can determine
Whether what is good for our personal
Life will also benefit or demean
Others. But if it is not criminal,
And our actions have no consequences
To deter us, then our self-interests
Will motivate us. Prison sentences
Are there to control us when we fail tests
Of good character however. Between
Self and others just keep the balance keen.

Credit Door Knock to FreeSFX
http://www.freesfx.co.uk/rx2/mp3s/9/9993_13601552
34.mp3

Storyteller: There was loud knock on the door and The Professor's attention was diverted from his lesson.

Professor: Come in!

[The Administration Staff]

Storyteller: Two administration staff enter, disrupting the lesson.

Admin 1: We would like to see this Student Mario Lanzones. Is he in this class?

Professor: Yes he is one of my students. What reason do you need to talk to him?

Admin 2: He texted our office with a long polysyllabic word 'disestablishmentarianism' and gave your name.

Admin 1: This is for the Sesquipedalian Award we announced to teachers this week.

Professor: What do you mean I have not used that word. Perhaps he misunderstood about who gets the award -- the teacher of the class or the student? You can question him yourselves although he might give you an

Equivocator's Excuses.

Student 1: In defence, It is my prerogative
To write fiction without naming sources.
Professor: Administration's interrogative
On a student's background and resources
Are to figure out the odd conundrum
Of a foreigner's knowledge.
Admin 1: Arresting
Though the phrases are, he came from humdrum
ESL class.
Student 1: I wrote them while texting,
Fighting the battle of hegemony!
Admin 2: We debated your equivocation
Of class, pointing out your lack of money.
Student 1: All I done was a change of vocation.
Professor: Debate this through Parliamentarianism
-- Antidisestablishmentarianism!

Storyteller: Both Administration staff stared with wonder at Professor Wroth and clapped!

Admin 2: Professor Helmut Wroth, congratulations! You just won the

Sesquipedalian Award right now!

Professor: Oh, it is meant for the teacher then not the students?

Admin 1: Yes you just used the longest word in the entire school antidisestablishmentarianism!

Admin 2: Now to win the Certificate of Recognition and the cash prize of $1000, please use it in a sentence which would express its meaning in context.

Professor: Wow, you put me on the hot seat! Okay here goes... The school Administration forms the establishment of education, so anyone who goes against them commits disestablishmentarianism, and if the school Administration then goes against that same person such as a foreign English Second Language student, it would be antidisestablishmentarianism!

Note: Class stands up to clap and cheer.
Credit FreeSFX Class Claps and Cheers
http://www.freesfx.co.uk/rx2/mp3s/1/902_124524963

<u>1.mp3</u>

<u>Storyteller:</u> The whole class of students stood up and clapped in happiness, along with the Administration staff who then handed Professor Wroth an envelope with the reward cash prize of one thousand dollars, plus a framed Certificate of the Sesquipedalian Award!

<u>Student 1:</u> Anti dis establish ment aria nism is difficult to pronounce and has eleven syllables!

Note: Female Administration staff laughs.
Credit FreeSFX Female laugh
<u>http://www.freesfx.co.uk/rx2/mp3s/5/5995_13358770</u>
<u>05.mp3</u>

<u>Storyteller:</u> The Administration staff laughed and left the ESL class.

<u>Professor:</u> Well class, it is time to conclude our lessons. Before the Administration's interruption of our class, I just want to reiterate the importance of education and conscience to determine our individual

intentions and actions and collectively our society's. This ability to analyze the past as it will influence our present and future can result in

Professor: Educated Guessing.
With my Master's, I like guesstimating
Outcomes in history with intuition,
Behaviour patterns, intimidating
Profiling of stereotypes. Paid tuition
In private universities instead
Of free public, allows educators
To choose curricula, living not dead
Authors. If new current indicators
Are cited in politics, reference
To dictators, Generals, Presidents,
In power can be studied. Influence
Present elections from past precedents!
The result? Voting becomes a science,
Leaders motives analyzed for conscience.

Professor: Before you all go out into the world again, I would like to say my

Last Words.

Professor: Students, whatever my ashes are worth,
Remember life is full of dialogues.
Thus, forgive me and my ego henceforth,
For filling your ears with my monologues.
Storyteller: The class clapped, applauding his final speech.

Note: Class stands to cheer and clap.
Credit FreeSFX Crowd Claps
http://www.freesfx.co.uk/rx2/mp3s/1/902_1245249631.mp3

Student 2: Sir, you are morbidly memorable!
Storyteller: The compliment made him blush like a peach.
Professor: Parting ways can be intolerable.
Storyteller: They lined up for his parting autograph.
Student 1: Thank you for all your lectures in English.
Professor: When you exit my class, my epigraph
Will ring in your ears! Avoid all foolish
Conversations. Speak with elocution.
Die by disease, not electrocution!

The Professor's Lessons

<u>Professor:</u> Class dismissed!

Note: Class continue standing with cheers and claps. Then start to exit his class room.
Credit FreeSFX
<u>http://www.freesfx.co.uk/rx2/mp3s/1/902_124524963 1.mp3</u>

<u>Storyteller:</u> Some students, Lei and Chiara line up for his autograph and take his photo with their cellphones.

<u>Poetess (unseen voice):</u> Professor, you have female and male fans waiting for your autograph and photograph! Words can woo listeners with the right voice...

Note: Signing autographs and taking pictures maybe takes a few minutes.

<u>Storyteller:</u> After The Students leave the room, The Administration staff return to discuss him and his class. Their concern was his reputation for eccentricity and being a

Hyperbolic Lecturer.

<u>Admin 1:</u> Congratulations again for

winning the award, although it was reported
you are

Admin 1: Impatient with students, did exe<u>crate</u>
Aloud.
<u>Professor:</u> Damn this ESL class! Dic<u>tion</u>
And Grammar of immigrants dese<u>crate</u>
The English language.
<u>Admin 2:</u> Your erudi<u>tion</u>
Angered.
<u>Professor:</u>   But I said, To err is hu<u>man</u>
Forgiving their ignorance.
<u>Admin 1:</u> Cocki<u>est</u>
Around pretty girls, you strutted – a <u>man</u>
Whose motto,'Errare humanum <u>est</u>'
Makes you popular with intellec<u>tuals</u>
Who pity those less blessed.
<u>Admin 2:</u> Intellig<u>ence</u>
Cause your exaggeration. Class ri<u>tuals</u>
Involve criticizing your rapt audi<u>ence</u>.
<u>Professor:</u> As teacher, I perform perfuncto<u>ry</u>
English lectures that are exempla<u>ry</u>!

<u>Storyteller:</u> Professor Helmut Wroth defended himself as usual despite the occasional criticism from The Administration. Education for him involved many subjects, to prepare for personal and professional areas in life, with analysis and criticism to improve intellect and problem solving skills. The Administration agreed his popularity with foreign ESL Students and their private funding of his public lectures made him a worthy member of their Faculty.

Note: The Administration staff and Professor continue discussion with speakers off at the same time that the bedroom set enters right and lights up.

Mini Set: a bedroom with pink canopy bed

<u>Storyteller:</u> While in her bedroom, Lei was thinking aloud of Professor Wroth in comparison and contrast to other men, seeing him as her

      Measuring Monument.
<u>Student 2:</u> I recall his clear lectures, insight<u>ful</u>

And interesting by comparison
To other teachers, I felt beautiful
Sitting and learning from him. This reason
Made me enjoy high school education.
He had a smart, suave style that could
seduce
My ignorance. Full of dedication,
I attended daily. He introduced
Us to use intellectual impression
With mild physical exasperation,
Sardonic humour, witty expression.
Striving for an A, in desperation,
I praised his ego, this male monument
Admitting he was my sole measurement!

Storyteller: Satisfied with Professor Wroth's explanations and rationalizations of his methods of teaching to foreign students, both Administration staff hear his cell phone ring and they say their good byes and leave his class room.

Credit FreeSFX Cell Phone Ring
http://www.freesfx.co.uk/rx2/mp3s/6/7268_13437356
51.mp3

Note: The Professor is now alone in the class room talking on his cell phone. His conversation with

Student 2 Lei is heard on speakers.

Professor: Hello? Helm here.

Storyteller: It is Student 2 calling him, lying in bed eating a box of chocolates, recalling him from high school in a

Tense Time Line.

Student 2: We had regular high school class meetings.

Do you remember? My Francophone tone?

Professor: Who are you? Do you expect nice greetings

After these years! What a surprise by phone!

Student 2: You forget me. No need to sound hostile.

Professor: I apologize, sorry, but which class?

Student 2: Must I explain? English. It's been awhile...

You are the one with long legs and tight ass?

Professor: Lei? What's your last name?

Student 2: It's not important.

Take a guess. Do you not recall my voice?
If a chocolate is left out, an ant
Tries to eat it, but a man beats the boys
And ant! Who would bother with this pretence?
Professor: We parted ways, hanging in mid-sentence...

Note: Pink and red flower petals fall down onto her bed from the ceiling. Curtains fall as he finally remembers who it is in the last line, turns off lights and heads out the door towards her bedroom in the mini set right side. Curtains are down with thunder and lightning sound effects before he enters it.

Credit FreeSFX Thunder
http://www.freesfx.co.uk/rx2/mp3s/1/943_1245800784.mp3

THE END

TRANSITION SCENE IN BETWEEN BOTH VERSIONS FOR STAGE PLAY:

When both Versions are performed as stage plays on the same afternoon / night, in between, the Transition Scene can be performed to explain the Collaboration between The Professor and The Poetess and the switch from The Censored to the Triple X Rated Full Versions. The Censored Version should be performed first in the afternoon, then the Transition Scene in the Cafe, then in the evening, The Full XXX Rated Version.

CENSORED VERSION
a variation for conventional morality

The Prostitute and The Gossip are NOT included, nor the Red Light District background screen. The left side of the stage only has a regular street white lamp and bench.

During Break, NO music and dancing included. The Students go outside in the left side park for Amusing Accents.

The Chairman and The Assistant too are not needed.

The Poetess appears only in the Censored Version. She communicates with The Professor via white board telepathy during the break instead of the wild music and dancing. She is also in the library before The Lovers are introduced. To bridge both Versions if played on the same afternoon to evening, in the Transition Scene at the Cafe, they meet and decide to collaborate as an experiment. In the XXX Version, only her spoken thoughts are heard but she does not appear at all.

White Board Telepathy

You are a spirit escaped from the glass!

[THE POETESS]
The Break
Scene: White Board Telepathy

Storyteller: During The Break, The Students go outside to the park to enjoy some fresh air and refreshments.

The Professor remains inside to eat his sandwich. He is interrupted by a strange sound and an image appearing on the white board.

Movie Adaptation:

Storyteller: Before starting his ESL class, The Professor is sitting at his desk alone. He is reading a newspaper and drinking coffee. He is interrupted by a strange sound and an image appearing on the white board.

Note: The Professor gets up from his desk and is staring surprised at the apparition projected on the white board.

Credit FreeSFX Alien Alarm

http://www.freesfx.co.uk/rx2/mp3s/7/8487_13533331
30.mp3

Storyteller: It is The Poetess, another Character in his mind, possibly a

Figment of Imagination.

Poetess: Professor, it is exami<u>nation</u>
Time. A multiple choice fun guess who
<u>game</u>.
Professor: You? A figment of imagi<u>nation</u>
Testing me? I refuse. Have you no sh<u>ame</u>?
Poetess: Master, guess who I am with your
sixth s<u>ense</u>.
Here are the choices: dead ghost, live
hu<u>man</u>
In another plane, succubus in m<u>en's</u>
Fantasies, a romantic dream wo<u>man</u>,
An alien from another gal<u>axy</u>,
A fictional character from a b<u>ook</u>?
Professor: A companion delivered by t<u>axi</u>?
I rarely fish in the sea off the h<u>ook</u>.
I prefer catching those within my c<u>lass</u>.
You are a spirit escaped from the g<u>lass</u>!

Storyteller: Both seemed to be
misunderstanding their telepathic
communication. They were unsure of who
the other was and whether there was any
significance or

Meaning In Conversation.

Poetess: Dead souls converse with a Ouija witch board.

I am alive but I hear every thought

Via telepathy. I use white board.

Professor: Dear are you not a student I once taught?

I think my memory does remember.

Poetess: Perhaps, long ago when life had meaning,

In English class, just another member.

Professor: But who are you? Not to be demeaning

If I forget your name. Conversation

Is limited in a class of silence...

Poetess: Yes, we listened without hesitation.

All ears, without uttering one sentence.

Professor: Normal class behaviour and school standard.

Learning by listening does not retard.

Storyteller: The argument about his method of teaching language and communication using a one way direction with the teacher doing all the talking while expecting his

class to listen silently, made her realize the
need for a

Role Reversal.

Poetess: Communication should have direction
With two ways between teacher and student.
Speaking requires equal conversation,
Like word battles, an armour with a dent.
Professor: Reversing roles requires enough knowledge.
I knew more than you before graduation
In high school. Did you attend a college?
Poetess: Only trade. A financial situation
Blocked my mental progress. Who could afford?
Professor: A loan, a job, savings, a scholarship.
Determination can melt ice for fjord,
Hidden icebergs can slice and sink a ship!
Poetess: All I have now is imagination.
Professor: With a dream, you can rule any nation.

Storyteller: The Poetess knew The

Professor was giving wise advice to gain
more education to achieve status in Society.
A teacher passes his knowledge to his
students, explaining why it went in a one
way direction. Their required silence was
not from being foreign students and racism,
but she vowed that

Diversity Is The Future.
Poetess: Traditional methods -- teaching
language
While listening in silence, does not work
For everyone. One must try to engage,
Others, not be an egocentric jerk.
Professor: Using slang words and
colloquialisms
That are North American? Did you learn
That on the streets? Careful about
schisms,
Ethnocentric racism... to discern
A foreign outsider by dialogue.
Open your mouth -- your words and strange
accent
Can cause ostracism...your epilogue!
Poetess: Diversity has a future ascent.
It will bring countries to world peace not

war.
Understanding people heals every scar.

Storyteller: To end their conversation,
Professor Wroth decided he would leave
and walk outside. He excused himself with
a

Polite Farewell.

Professor: The intermission break is almost
done.
I have to bid you a polite farewell.
Poetess: Outside the fresh air awaits with
the sun.
I will release you from my ghoulish spell.
Poems and lectures are all words, written
Or spoken as sweet poetry or prose.
Which form will the speaker use to smitten
A listener, does each smell like a rose?

Note: She smells a red rose.

Professor: I am tired of your odd puzzling
riddles.
Find someone else to play with mentally.
I have a Master Degree. Who fiddles

With me shall lose in the final <u>tally</u>.

<u>Poetess:</u>   Good-bye Wroth! Future answers lie in d<u>reams</u>.

Past problems lay silent like unheard sc<u>reams</u>.

Note: The transmission ends with the same strange noise as The Professor exits the class room by the front door.

Credit FreeSFX Alien Noise

<u>http://www.freesfx.co.uk/rx2/mp3s/7/8487_1353333130.mp3</u>

Transition Scene Between Both Versions
Scene: Experiment Agreement

Mini Set Right: a cafe with 3 coffee tables, spotlight 1 table and 2 chairs

<u>Storyteller:</u> The scene opens with The Poetess waiting at the table drinking coffee checking her cell mobile phone. The Professor received a text from her to meet at the Cafe. She has a notebook and is thinking and writing notes while waiting. He arrives and recognizes her from their previous telepathic communication on the

white board in the ESL class room.

Professor: What? You again? How did you get my mobile cell phone number?

Poetess: Via telepathy of course. A wireless telephone uses the same airwaves!

Professor: (sits) We have met before in reality. I gave you a B in English if I recall correctly.

Poetess: Unfortunately, you did not give me an A. But I forgive you. It made you memorable strangely...

Professor: (laughs) I only give As to those who study and deserve it.

Poetess: Hmm... I suppose we use language in different ways and levels...poetry and prose. Have you ever included both in class?

Professor: Curriculum Collaboration?
Mixing nonsense with logic and reason
Would confuse students, add to ignorance!
Poetess: It is not a crime, committing
treason
Against the Queen's language! Rhyme can
entrance
With rhythm. Words have an intelligence
That combine wisdom, meaning, and
knowledge.
Professor: I know all that! I teach with
diligence --
Language, so precisely, my cutting edge
Sharpens minds not dulls. Critical thinking
Builds successful careers not illusions.
Poetess: Starving artists, luxury ships
sinking,
Romantic losers lost in delusions...
Professor: Failure would destroy
collaboration.
Evidence supports corroboration.

Poetess: But what if

Poetess: Edutainment Enlightens?
Some schools study the craft of poetry.
Professor: I teach language and all its
precise rules!
In the Garden of Eden, which fruit tree
Is chosen Life or Knowledge? Naked fools
Wandering around full of innocence?
Poetess: Adam and Eve lacked sex
education.
The snake saw no need for such sweet
pretence.
But God cast them out from their vacation.
Professor: Public reaction to entertainment
Contradicts a formal institution.
Poetess: It depends on a mutual
agreement
Like choosing marriage or prostitution.
Mixing both would explain human nature
Wild and tamed combined would deem one
mature.

Professor: This could lead to a breakdown
of

Professor: Sexual Morality!
Art loosens people's primitive instincts.

Freedom to create without restriction,
Whereas education has its precincts,
Strict boundaries full of rules constriction.
Poetess: Rules outdated need to be updated.
The world is full of human corruption
That schools have to prepare students fated
To doom if lacking knowledge. What option
Can you offer them when they are outside?
Professor: School is not a sheltered Eden Garden!
Values of right from wrong in sex deride
Some types of sexuality, but heathen
Like entertaining with immoral ways.
Poetess: The popularity of a trend sways...

Professor: Remember too the new rule in Education

Professor: Regulation 274?
Diversity versus seniority...
Hiring policies... older is wiser...
The majority rules minority...
Poetess: Racial intelligence exists. Why sir?

Now that English is a global language,
Why regret passing on knowledge in schools,
And books? Youth learns skills and concepts from age.
Professor: I have no regrets like other dumb fools!
I was hired to teach, did my job, got paid,
Mortgage and house, retired with a pension.
Poetess: No need to argue words. Your point is laid
To rest. I learned from you despite tension.
Professor: I teach foreign students whatever race
Or culture, I do not judge mind by face.

Poetess: Media Brainwashing!
People have been brainwashed by mass media.
Professor: An expert in mass communication,
I mastered skills and encyclopedia.
Morality controlled fornication.
Poetess: Schools are behind the times.
Television

And movies are violent, sexual, corrupt.

Professor: People I would sneer at with derision.

Such students are kicked out, those who disrupt.

Poetess: Diversity increases cultural Clashes, but English is used as a bridge.

Professor: Degrees lift minds and souls from gutteral.

Morality is the dividing ridge.

Poetess: The Church, The School, The Media, which controls

The Masses? Ask the bridge ogres and trolls?

Professor: We shall see... if we try an experiment allowing diversity and the outside world's corruption, freedom of choice in sexuality to influence our behaviour as education has tried. Rules are broken because they restrict human nature and its primitive instincts. Mind over body and body over mind... I teach a lot of foreign students and wonder what they have learned to use in life and career.

Poetess: The school a bastion of morality

invaded and corrupted gradually from outside and within ourselves. Sexuality a primitive instinct can beat civilized morality...

Professor: ...for some individuals. It has to feel right for self and society. One has to feel comfortable with taking risks despite curiosity.

Poetess: Agreed. Let us shake hands on this and put pens on paper for our autographed signatures.

Note: Both shake hands and then sign a document in agreement. Spotlight turns off.

Movie adaptation:
Note: the film changes from black and white to coloured at the park bench and street lamp scene.

Storyteller: As The Professor returns to the school, he stops puzzled and looks around at the park bench and street lamp outside, where the Red Light District has mysteriously set up in the background. He recalls the cafe conversation with The Poetess, but hurries to school to start his ESL class.

Before The Lovers
Scene: Library Loneliness
Mini Set Right: a library with desk and laptop
Back Screen: wall with books

<u>Storyteller:</u> After their telepathic communication, The Poetess is at her home library and desk with laptop computer, talking aloud to herself.

<u>Poetess:</u>   Alone In Peace
Drinking coffee in my home while <u>writing</u>
I listen to poetry through ster<u>eo</u>.
Peace and quiet alone without <u>writhing</u>
And turmoil with a partner. To stare, <u>oh</u>
Whose cruel eyes are missing to crit<u>icize</u>
My soul and mind? I listen to ro<u>mance</u>
With its doomed patterns, despite moans and <u>sighs</u>.
A lot of couples part ways from the <u>man's</u>
Indifference and woman's cont<u>rolling</u>
Grip. Recalling my own past love aff<u>airs</u>,
They wanted freedom and friends, a <u>rolling</u>
Hidden camera for drama in p<u>airs</u>.
Being alone suits me. Since I rel<u>eased</u>

Them, I can now finally rest in p<u>eace</u>...

But tortured by the

<u>Poetess:</u>   Loneliness Of Lovelessness.
Curiously, poetry breeds analg<u>esia</u>;
Perhaps blocking pain caused by
lone<u>liness</u>.
Yet some recall, forgo this amn<u>esia</u>,
Which heals the worn soul with its
love<u>liness</u>.
Oh that lone despair were epheme<u>ral</u>
Vanishing quick, not plaguing the tim<u>id</u>.
Would we in solitary cereb<u>ral</u>
Pursuits advance toward the more viv<u>id</u>
Aspects of life? Vibrant is life's strong
v<u>oice</u>,
Verdant as forest green, natu<u>ral</u>
And vast. Shy cowards and meek hear the
n<u>oise</u>
Ordering death of life, non-libe<u>ral</u>,
Confining, full of shushing balderd<u>ash</u>,
Cremating both Youth and Elder to <u>ash</u>!

Time passes without love and yet thoughts
and wishes remain to be written by

Note: Students slowly return to the class room.

Poetess: Losers In Love.
Many poems and songs have been written,
By those who experienced unrequited
Love. Struck by strangers arrows, and smitten
Silent remain in desperate quietude.
When the subject of one's secret affection
Has no mutual feeling nor interest
Then a feigned shield full of affectation
Protects one's heart, soul, and body to rest.
But the mind continues to expressions,
Trying to understand one's suffering
In song or poem, leaving impressions
To the public. Artistic offering
Of a tortured soul who has lost all hope
Of winning love, but continues to cope.

There are other subjects who inspire,
ordinary people who trigger poetry,
becoming a

Poetess: Domestics Muse.
We honour in rhyme, muse emeritus
Those worthy to incite our souls in forte.

Poetry sublime, not wordy de<u>tritus</u>,
Inspires, delicious as a fancy <u>torte</u>!
Shall we joust in some verbal tour<u>nament</u>,
Arousing ourselves from cata<u>lepsy</u>
To decorate a brilliant or<u>nament</u>?
Clear bouts of poetic epi<u>lepsy</u>
Uplifts us to literacy gent<u>eel</u>.
In tense, we in lyrical conf<u>erence</u>,
Aspire to build poems, bold towers of <u>feel</u>,
Pyramids of romantic rev<u>erence</u>.
How fantasies enflame in dom<u>estic</u>
People, a grandeur superb, ma<u>jestic</u>!

Talking to myself again, lost in imagination.
But sometimes it seems I am not always so
alone while writing, as if an invisible
collaborator corresponds like my

<u>Poetess:</u>   Secret Ghost Writer?
Telepathy seems to exist betw<u>een</u>
Me and a male who co-writes dia<u>logues</u>.
His inner voice developing a sc<u>ene</u>
In poems. If we keep notes and journal
<u>logs</u>,
It could last years of collabor<u>ation</u>.
Several sonnets were written a<u>long</u>

With him, for characters conversation.
He felt so close in mind like we belong
Together on the same vibration waves!
It is great to have his understanding
Adding meaning to poems. Whoever paves
The path of enlightenment demanding
The readers attention is a Master!
How to thank him for being a ghost writer?

Storyteller: The Poetess tired of her solitary
monologue, decides to go for a walk
outside.

Note: Poetess walks out of the library. Next set is
for The Lovers.

At the Conclusion's End, Student 2 is in the
park bench not her bedroom while talking
on cell phone. Make sure to change words
from bedroom to park. Professor steps out
and sits beside her on the bench and they
continue to talk but with speakers off.
Curtains fall.

THE END

Movie Adaptation

While Credits are playing, the Professor is at home writing notes in his notebook for his lectures. He lives alone in a house.

For the movie, the order of the versions to show both the Censored to XXX rated:
1. Censored Break with White Board Telepathy Scene between Professor and Poetess; after this he walks out, passes a simple bench and park and he gets a text.
2. Transition Experiment Agreement Cafe Scene meeting in the coffee shop between Professor and Poetess who sent him a text. They agree to an experiment showing how morality, sexuality and diversity can change school. He walks back to the school but this time the park and bench are now in the Red Light District set up beside the school.*
3. XXX Version with Language Lessons and first half of Character Lessons
4. XXX Afternoon Break with Primitivism Party music and wild dancing
5. Chairman's Consternation Scene
6. Library Loneliness Scene of Poetess
7. Continue Character Lessons with The

Lovers

8. Conclusion after the Administration
leave him, call from Student 2 in bedroom

* Note: Credits,1 & 2 in black/white film, then colour
from 3 to ending